BITTER

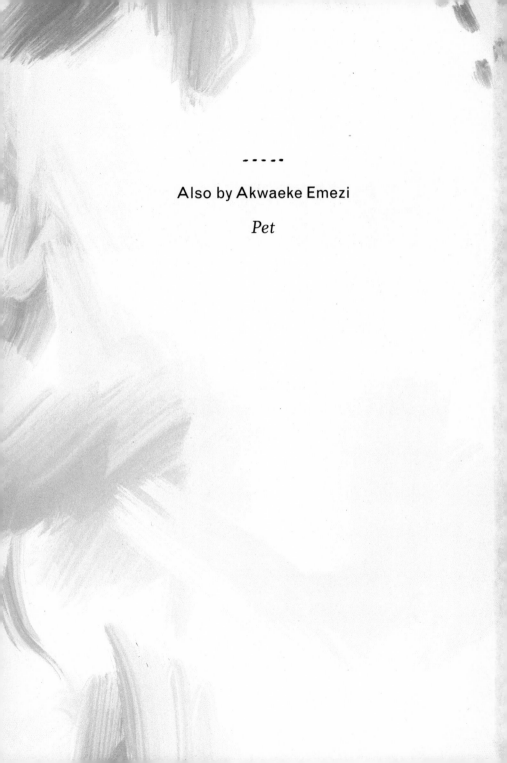

- - - --

Also by Akwaeke Emezi

Pet

BITTER

AKWAEKE EMEZI

ALFRED A. KNOPF
NEW YORK

Still and always, for Toyin Salau.
You deserved a better world.

CHAPTER 1

- - - - - - - - - - - - -

Bitter had no interest in the revolution.

She was seventeen, and she thought it was ridiculous that adults wanted young people to be the ones saving the world, as if her generation was the one that had broken everything in the first place. It wasn't her business. She was supposed to have had a childhood, a whole world waiting for her when she grew up, but instead kids her age were the ones on the front lines, the ones turned into martyrs and symbols that the adults praised publicly but never listened to because their greed was always louder and it was easier to perform solidarity than to actually *do* the things needed for change. It didn't matter. None of it fucking mattered.

Bitter sat in her room and ignored the shouts from outside her window, the stomping of feet, the rhythmic chants, thousands of throats swelling to the same song. Lucille was a brutal city to live in. There had been mass shootings at the public schools, at the movie theaters, at the shopping

I

centers. Everyone knew someone else who had died from something they didn't have to die from. Too many people had seen others die, even if it was in frantic livestreams and videos, witnesses risking their lives and freedoms to record the cops and their gleeful atrocities. Too many mothers had buried their children under a lethally indifferent administration. All of Bitter's friends were sick of it, and rightfully so. The world was supposed to have gotten better, not become even more violent, rank with more death. It was no wonder the people took to the streets, masses swallowing the roads and sidewalks, because in a world that wanted you dead, you had to scream and fight for your aliveness.

Sometimes Bitter wished she didn't live so close to the center of the city, though; every protest in Lucille seemed to stream past this building, the sound leaking up the walls, levering its way over her windowsill, stubbornly penetrating the glass and blinds and curtains. Bitter wished she could soundproof it all away. She curled up in the large gray armchair pushed against the wall as far from the window as her room would allow and bent her head over her sketchbook, turning up the old-school music in her headphones and worrying at the steel ring in her lower lip. The metal was cool against her tongue, and Big Freedia's voice fell into her ears over an accelerating beat as Bitter mouthed the words along, trying to match the speed, her pencil making quick,

2

strong strokes over the paper. A mouth grew under her hand, a tail and a sleek neck, smooth round scales packed neatly on top of each other, curve after curve peeking out. She made its eyes as dark as she could, small black stones nearly weighing through the paper.

Sometimes, when she had music filling her ears and paper spreading at her fingers, Bitter could almost feel the bubble she was building, as if it was tangible, a shield that would protect her better than her weak windows. If she got it just right, maybe she could block out everything else entirely. Maybe when the stomps and chants five floors down on the street turned into screams and people running, the bubble could block out the other sounds that Bitter knew would come with it—the clank and hiss of canisters, the attack dogs barking, the dull heaviness of water cannons spitting wet weight on flesh. On the bad days, there was gunfire, an inhuman staccato. Sometimes the streets were hosed off afterward. Bitter frowned and bent closer to her drawing, adding a crest of spikes. It looked like a dragon now, which was fine, but it just wasn't right. She ripped out the sheet from her sketchbook and crumpled it into a messy ball, tossing it aside. She'd have to start again, pay more attention to what she was pulling out of the page.

Almost immediately, she felt a brief pang of regret at having crumpled up the dragon. Maybe she could've tried to work with it instead, but Bitter knew the answer even as she asked the question. There were things she could draw and then there were *things* she could draw, and when the streets were loud the way they were this evening, only the second sort of thing would do. Only the second sort of thing could make her feel a little less lonely.

She was about to start sketching again when her door swung open and someone stepped in. Bitter pulled off her headphones, pissed at the interruption, but the visitor raised her hands in peace. "Don't even start, Bitter—I knocked! You never hear anything with those headphones on." She was a tall girl in a neon-pink hijab, which framed her soft face. Her lashes were a mile long, and tiny iridescent stickers were scattered over her cheekbones. Bitter relaxed. "Hi, Blessing. Wha's the scene?"

Without her headphones, the sounds from the street seemed to fill up her room. Blessing sat on the bed, stretching her legs out in front of her. Her jeans and hoodie were covered with colorful doodles, flowers and suns and rainbows. It was aggressively adorable, and Bitter hid a smile. The two girls had been friends for years, since they'd both come to this school and started living in the dorms, small bedrooms lined up next to each other. Blessing had been the one who shaved Bitter's head for the first time, dark tufts of hair falling in clouds around them, and Bitter had kept her curls cropped close since then, because she could, because here she was as free as she'd ever been. They both knew how special that was. Blessing had been in and out of queer shelters since her parents kicked her out, but then a social worker found her and told her the same thing Bitter had been told—that there was a private boarding school called Eucalyptus, that it was for young artists and she'd been selected, that none of the students had to worry about paying for it. All they had to do was graduate.

It made no sense. No one knew who owned the school, only that it was full of kids like Bitter and Blessing who had been found and brought somewhere safe. They all had the same story of the first time they walked into Eucalyptus: the rush of relief and security they'd felt when they met Miss Virtue, the extraordinarily tall woman who ran the school. Miss Virtue had a deep voice, a shock of steel hair, and the most eerie gray eyes, and she was always dressed in the sharpest suits they'd ever seen, not to mention that she was the kindest person they'd ever met. All the kids ignored that first rush of relief because they'd learned the hard way that you couldn't trust first impressions, but after a while, they also learned that Eucalyptus was different, and that was because of Miss Virtue. You couldn't help but feel safe around her, not because she was soft or anything, but because there was something behind her dark skin, something terrifying that

5

leaked through her gray eyes and made everyone uncomfortably aware that her kindness was a deliberate choice. It also made them feel safe, like she would go to horrific lengths to protect them, and that was what they needed, someone who believed they were worth burning the world down for.

Still, all the students were curious about who Miss Virtue worked for, whose money ran Eucalyptus, how and why they had been chosen to attend, but there were no answers for these questions. Even the hacker kids couldn't find a trail that would explain any of it. Bitter didn't care. Eucalyptus was safe, and that was all that mattered, especially when you knew what other options were out there. Bitter had bounced around foster homes since she was a baby, ending up with a steady foster family when she was eight, and she had removed all memories of the years before that, on purpose, because she needed to stay sane and some memories were like poison.

Her new foster family had known her biological parents, but they hadn't liked Bitter very much. *Your father was a monster,* the woman there used to say, *and you're going to end up nowhere. It kill your mother, you know—that's why she give you this name, that's why she did die when you was a baby, you born with a curse.* They were religious, and they didn't like how loud Bitter was, how she stared at them with unflinching eyes, how she liked to draw almost as much as she liked to talk and challenge and yell. It was just Bitter and the woman and her husband, both from her mother's island, both stern and cold, and while they weren't as cruel to Bitter as she felt they could've been, her whole life in that house had been one continuous wilting. When she'd pierced her lip, the woman had slapped her so hard that new blood fell against Bitter's teeth, so she'd started running away like she was taking small calm trips. Inevitably, she was found and brought back, found and brought back, until the Eucalyptus social worker found her and asked her if she wanted to leave, and yes, hell yes, she wanted to leave. And the woman and the man came and said goodbye and preached at her for a little bit, told her things about herself Bitter had stopped believing, and then the social worker took her away, and then there was Eucalyptus and Miss Virtue and Blessing, and Bitter had all the friends she could roll with, all the time to draw that she wanted, and a room with a door she could lock, even if it was all too close to the city center.

"We're going out to the park later to smoke, if you wanna come," Blessing said. "After the protests die down. I know you don't like to be near all that shit."

Bitter tucked her feet under her legs and put her sketchbook aside. "Who's *we*?"

Blessing shrugged. "Me, Alex, and some new kid she's decided to drag along."

Alex was Blessing's girlfriend, a sculptor who'd arrived at Eucalyptus a few months ago with a rolling trunk full of tools. Her lean arms were covered with little scars from burns and cuts because she worked with metal, and a story spread around the school pretty fast that she'd been part of Assata, the young rebels behind most of the protests and direct action, the ones who faced down the police with flaming flags and holy ash. Rumor had it that Alex had been recruited by Eucalyptus, had walked away from the front lines to come to their school and make art. That direction was unusual; it was more likely that the school lost students who ran off to join Assata, not the other way around. Bitter wanted to ask Alex if it was all true, and if so, why she'd left, but it wasn't the kind of thing you just asked someone like that. Not when Assata kids were turning up dead in their own cars with bullet holes in their heads and suicide lies in their police reports, not when their families were being spied on, when the archivists were being thrown in prison for documenting the horrors happening in their communities. You kept it quiet, you kept it as rumors and whispers. You just didn't ask.

"Okay." A smoke in the park sounded great to Bitter. It would be chill by then, no more crowds and stomping, and the stars would be out.

"Aight, cool." Blessing stood up. "I'll leave you alone with your drawing. I know how you get."

8

Bitter rolled her eyes. "Whatever." She was already flipping her sketch pad open by the time the door closed behind Blessing's chuckle. Her friends could always tell when she was in a mood, and they knew that drawing would help. Bitter slipped her headphones back on and decided to try for something simpler.

Under her pencil, a round figure stretched out over an hour, gossamer wings and multiple eyes. She kept it small and tight, a mutant ladybug that could fit in her palm. Then she painted slow watercolors over it in shades of gray and black. When it was time for the finish, Bitter got up and locked her door first. No one could ever see this part. She reached for a tack from her desk and stabbed the tip of her thumb with it, watching the bead of blood that bloomed forth before squeezing it gently onto the drawing. The red seeped into the monochrome of the tiny creature, and Bitter sucked at the wound on her thumb to stop the bleeding. She touched the drawing with her other hand and called it the way she'd been doing since she was a little kid.

Come out nuh, she said in her head. *Come out and play.*

Even though she'd seen this happen countless times before, it still looked unbelievably cool when the creature wriggled out from the paper, tearing it open. It shook itself on the sketch pad, and Bitter grinned.

Welcome, she said.

Her little creatures couldn't talk, and they always vanished after a day or two, but Bitter could *feel* them, and they made her feel less alone, chittering across her room. This one climbed onto her palm when she held her hand out and bounced up and down on its thin legs. Bitter laughed.

Yuh real cute for an ugly thing, she told it.

It wriggled and flapped its delicate wings, lifting into the air with a buzz. She watched it fly around her bookshelves, checking out her plants, its body a dark smudge in the air with a glint of blood red when the light caught it. There was always a deep calm that spread over Bitter when she brought her work to life. It made her bubble into something real— it was a particular magic that she shared with no one else, and if this was so unquestionably real, then everything that was out there didn't have to be. *This* was her favorite world to live in.

The creature landed on the windowsill and bumped against it a few times, buzzing impatiently. Bitter sighed and walked over to it.

What, you want to go outside?

It flew up again, whirling around her head before settling on the back of her hand. Bitter lifted it up to eye level.

All right, she said. *Come back before yuh disappear, okay?*

It vibrated on her hand and flapped its wings again.

Yeah, yeah. That's what allyuh does say. Bitter smiled and opened the window, watching her creation fly away and vanish into the night air. The stars were out and the moon was a dripping peach in the sky. She stared out at Lucille for a moment, then closed her window and pulled on her hoodie. It was time to go find Blessing.

Bitter was expecting to find Alex and Blessing tangled up together on Blessing's bed like they always were these days, cuddling and giggling and being disgustingly cute, but when Bitter stepped into Blessing's room, her best friend was alone and ready to head out.

"We'll meet them in the park," she told Bitter, handing her a small bottle of rum.

Bitter nodded and took a sip before slipping it into her pocket. "You bring the speakers?"

"Nah, Alex said it's better to lay low tonight. Too much tension from earlier." They left Eucalyptus through a side gate that shouldn't have been open, except that the school had given up on trying to keep it closed, since the locks kept getting broken no matter how sophisticated they got. Eucalyptus kids liked nothing more than a challenge.

The streets around the park were littered with debris from the earlier protests, trampled cardboard and a few water bottles leaking milk. Some of the Assata kids were cleaning up, and seeing it irritated Bitter. There wouldn't *be* anything to clean up if they just stayed home in the first place. She made a face and gave them a wide berth as she and Blessing entered the park, but one of them caught her expression and straightened, spikes swinging from knots at the ends of her purple braids.

Bitter swore under her breath. "Oh shit, that's Eddie."

Blessing looked over curiously. "Homegirl from the summer? Didn't you ghost her?"

"That's not the point." Bitter tried to hide behind Blessing, but it was too late.

"Look," Eddie called out, her eyes fixed on Bitter. "It's some basic Eucalyptus bitches! What did y'all do today, draw some stick figures while the real ones were out here making change happen?" Her mouth was twisted in challenge, and she had a mottled bruise around her left eye, a scabbed cut slicing through her eyebrow.

Anger shot through Bitter. "You feelin' real bold, oui?" Blessing grabbed her arm to hold her back, but Eddie was already dropping her trash and walking toward them.

"Oh, I got time today," she yelled from across the street. "Let's go, come on."

Bitter shook free of Blessing and took a step forward, ready to face down Eddie, but she hesitated when she saw who was pulling up behind the girl. She recognized him as one of Assata's leaders, a tall blue-black boy in a wheelchair, the one with a voice like a prophet. He was always organizing, seeming to be both a backbone and an amplifier for the chanting masses whose noise kept pouring through her windows. His presence was heavily intimidating, enough to stop Bitter in her tracks.

"Back off, Eddie," he commanded.

Eddie whipped around but deflated as soon as she saw who it was. "I'm just fucking with them, Ube."

Ube cut his eyes at her. "Focus on your own shit. They ain't your business." She glared at him, then at the girls, before stalking off with the others, picking up the frontline debris.

"We eh need your help," Bitter snapped.

Ube stared coolly back at her. "Who says I was helping you?"

He turned and left before Bitter could form a retort, and Blessing laughed.

"I like him," she said.

Bitter rolled her eyes. "You just think he cute."

"Aw, come on. He's doing good work out here. All the Assata kids are."

Bitter didn't say anything. Blessing had become even more pro-Assata since she started dating Alex, and it was something Bitter was too scared to ask her about. What if the rumors about Alex were true and she was still loyal to Ube and his comrades? What if Alex decided to leave Eucalyptus and go back to Assata? What if she took Blessing with her? Bitter didn't want her oldest friend out there in the screams and fire. Assata kids *died*. She wanted Blessing within the school walls, in the safety it felt like only Eucalyptus could provide.

They came up to their favorite oak tree, with the graffiti-soaked picnic table and benches laid out underneath. Alex was sitting on the table in her usual all black, small keloids glinting dark on her wrist as she lit a joint. Her eyes shone behind her pink glasses when she saw Blessing, and she swung her legs down, stretching out her arms. "Hey, baby," she crooned, and Bitter watched Blessing melt into her girl-friend's arms, their mouths meeting like home. She glanced away, annoyed at the spike of jealousy that burst through her. It wasn't that she wanted Alex or Blessing—not like that, at least—but watching how they clicked stung. Bitter had dated a lot of people at Eucalyptus, and none of it had ever felt the way Blessing talked about Alex.

It didn't matter, she reminded herself. None of this was real enough to matter.

She stepped around them and climbed up on the picnic table, pulling a lighter out of her back pocket. The lovebirds were murmuring to each other, soft giggles interspersed between the words. Bitter tried not to roll her eyes. She hated when couples acted like they were the only ones there, like their feelings could protect them from the rest of the world. The lighter flame crackled as she flicked it on and off, and then she heard a breath behind her. Bitter jumped off the table, singeing her finger as she backed away.

There was someone else there, sitting at the end of one of the benches.

"What the fuck?" Bitter shouted.

Blessing and Alex snapped their necks around, their eyes sharp and alert, Alex's hand reaching for something in her waistband. Bitter wished she'd brought something with her—pepper spray, or a knife, anything. This was Lucille—you never knew who was in the shadows.

Blessing took a step forward and frowned. "Bitch," she said to Alex, "ain't that the new kid?"

Alex dropped her hand and huffed out a breath. "Bruh! Can you not sit there like a fucking lurker? That shit is creepy as fuck."

Bitter stepped next to Blessing as the boy at the edge of the bench stood up and walked toward them, his hands held out in apology. "Sorry, sorry," he said. "I was falling asleep small. I didn't mean to frighten anyone." He had a gap between his two front teeth, a wide mouth, and long eyelashes.

Bitter tried not to stare at the way his dark skin gleamed over his cheekbones, the broad slope of his shoulders, the cut of his arms, the way his chest stretched out his T-shirt.

"You have a bad habit of sneaking up on people," Blessing complained. "You did the same shit this afternoon when we met!"

The boy ran a hand through his short dreadlocks. "It wasn't on purpose! I'm just quiet." He shrugged and hooked his thumbs into the pockets of his jeans, then turned to Bitter. "I'm very sorry I startled you," he said, his voice gentling.

His accent was from somewhere else, somewhere warm. Bitter felt her pulse quicken as his eyes met hers—there was something tender about how he was looking at her, and she wondered if he looked at the rest of the world the same way. The boy held out his hand, and when Bitter slid her palm into his, part of her chest exhaled without her, a locked fraction of her spine unwound and clicked free. She could hear Blessing's voice as if it was filtered, and the boy's gap-toothed smile was breaking open again, but this time it was just for her, and it felt like it was happening in slow motion, a prolonged dazzling.

"Bitter," Blessing was saying, "this is Aloe."

CHAPTER 2

- - - - - - - - - - -

The first creature didn't need that much blood.

Bitter had been six or seven then, inside one of the lost years, in a house she didn't remember. She'd been hiding under a table and drawing with crayons, a yellow butterfly with lopsided wings, when someone started yelling and she jerked, the paper slicing a thin cut into her thumb. Bitter had whimpered, then shoved the sound down into her little belly because it would all get so much worse if they heard her cry. She put the drawing down, and a whisper of blood smudged across the butterfly's wing. Bitter stuck her thumb in her mouth and watched with wide eyes as her drawing shimmered and the butterfly lifted off the page, fluttering around her in crayoned silence. Maybe she should have been afraid, but even as young as she was then, Bitter had been alone for too long and she'd seen much more terrifying things than a drawing deciding to come to life. Her butterfly felt like a friend, for the half hour it stayed with Bitter under the table before dissolving into sunshine dust.

It was a long time before she tried it again. It had taken on the texture of a dream by then; she wasn't sure if it had really happened. The second time, she was in a foster family's attic, hiding again, this time with a ragged sketchbook someone had given her in an in-between house, an in-between time. Bitter backed into a corner of the attic and scraped her shoulder on a nail, gasping at the sting of pain. This house had a boy cousin visiting. He liked to corner her when the foster parents were out, grab her by her hair, and so far, the attic was the only place he hadn't come looking for her. Bitter reached up and touched the scratch, then stared at the blood that came back smeared against her fingertip. A memory of a clumsy yellow butterfly that had been a comfort flitted through her mind. She pulled out her sketchbook and held the page close to her face so she could see in the dim attic light as she drew a small cat, simple lines and quick circles. Bitter poked at her shoulder again and rubbed the touch of blood into her drawing. She stared at it, her breath held in her chest, her heart pounding with anticipation. The drawing blurred and shimmered, then the cat stretched and trotted off the page, its whiskers wobbling as it walked. Bitter stifled a delighted squeal. It hadn't been a dream! This time the cat and Bitter played together for a few quiet hours before it curled up and faded into gray, then nothing. That was okay. It made Bitter a little sad, but she was used to loss.

The drawings had helped Bitter get through the years before she came to Eucalyptus, and once she had her own space, a steady haven to sleep and breathe in, Bitter slowly learned what it was like to draw when she felt safe. It was a strange feeling, but a good one. She didn't like to think about what would happen after graduation if she left Eucalyptus. Miss Virtue always told them that they didn't have to leave if they didn't want to, that there would always be jobs at Eucalyptus for its students. You could teach, you could do something, anything else. Bitter wondered if it was the easy way out, never leaving. Just staying in the bubble forever, just you and your art. It didn't sound half bad, but Blessing always pushed back against it. The morning after they'd been at the park, Bitter brought it up again. "I think I gonna have a talk with Miss Virtue about job openings, for afterwards."

"Eucalyptus isn't everything," Blessing pointed out. "What about the rest of Lucille?"

Bitter shrugged. "It's all on fire. What's left out there?"

"Oh, come on. You can't throw away a whole city just because it's broken."

They were in Blessing's room, the television playing

muted cartoons on the wall as the girls shared a bag of sour gummi worms. Bitter glanced out of the window and shook her head.

"It's more than broken, Blessing. Actually," she corrected herself, "it's not even broken. It's doing what it was meant to do: protecting those rich motherfuckers and killing everyone else. Allyuh acting like you could change that."

"We *can* change it!" Blessing's eyes were bright with something Bitter couldn't find in herself. "What do you think Assata is out there fighting for? What do you think the old-timers fought for? We can *make* the mayor and the council listen to us."

Bitter laughed, and the sound echoed her name. "This is Lucille. The mayor and the council eh matter. You and me both know who matters here."

A flash of anger passed over Blessing's face, but it wasn't directed at Bitter. "Yeah," she said. "Dian Theron and his fucking money."

Bitter didn't blame her friend for the snaking hatred that hissed through her voice. Dian Theron was a billionaire who owned everything that mattered in Lucille, and everyone knew that the mayor and the council answered to him. That was the power money had: it mattered over people; it could put a bullet into the head of anyone who was too loud, who found out too much. Theron was always in the papers, making headlines with the obscene amounts of wealth he was hoarding. His face was burned into Bitter's memory: the pasty skin and thin blond hair, the hawk nose, the unnaturally white teeth. When she thought of greed, she thought of Theron.

And yes, Bitter just wanted to make her art and mind her own business, but she could agree with Assata and Blessing that Theron was evil. It was impossible to be a billionaire and be good. You couldn't make that kind of money without hurting people, without stealing from them, exploiting them, making them suffer while you accumulated wealth that was impossible to spend in this lifetime. Just sitting on it for nothing, while others were struggling to stay alive. He could have used that money to do so much for the people of Lucille, used his influence to make the administration change how they treated their citizens, but Theron didn't care. It worked better for his profit margins the way it was. The whole thing was selfish and cruel, and it made Bitter more angry than she had space for, because she knew what selfish and cruel felt like on the receiving end, she had years she couldn't remember because of it. She had suffering knitted into her bones, and on her worst days, she tried not to think about how much she had in common with her mother.

"Theron isn't above the law," Blessing said, and it shot irritation through Bitter. Why did people insist on being this naive? Did it just make them feel better to think that they could control what was happening, as if they had any power? As if the world was just slightly off course, and with enough sweat and will they could push it back on track?

"Theron *is* the law," she snapped. "Or you forgetting how money does work in Lucille?"

Blessing gave her a patient look. "There are some things that matter more than money," she said.

Bitter kissed her teeth. "Tell that to the mayor dem." She shoved the bag of gummi worms back at Blessing and fought the urge to get up and leave, go back to her room, draw something that made more sense than this world. Her skin was crawling.

"Okay, okay. Let's change the subject." Blessing could always tell when Bitter had reached her breaking point. "Can we talk about the new boy?"

A flush wrapped around Bitter's neck. "Aloe? What about him?"

"Girl, I see how you two were looking at each other! You feeling him, huh?"

Bitter rolled her eyes. "He real cute, sure. Maybe we hook up once or twice, but that's it."

Blessing shook her head. "I don't think he's that type, Bitter."

"He's a guy. There's no other type."

"Nah, I think he's different. You know what his skill is?"

"I didn't ask." She'd been too shaken to think of it last night, but Bitter was curious. It was the first question Eucalyptus kids usually asked each other: What's your skill? Do you paint, draw, sculpt, sing? Do you work with clay, metal, tech, fabric? She tried to imagine what the new boy's medium was. Maybe he took photos or wrote stories.

Blessing grinned. "He's a sound artist."

Bitter raised an eyebrow. "Really?"

"Yup. He's looking into the healing properties of sound, the ways it can affect our brains and shit. You should ask him for a sound bath."

"I not asking him for shit."

Blessing leered at her friend. "Ask him for a kiss. You know you want to."

Bitter snatched the bag of gummi worms back. "You eating too much damn sugar. I cutting you off."

"That's how I got Alex, you know. You just gotta say what you want."

"It's different with girls," Bitter replied, biting into a blue worm. "Guys doh like it when you act like you want it."

"Then you don't need to be fucking with guys like that. We're people too—we got needs and whatnot."

Bitter cast a sidelong glance at Blessing. "How things going with Alex?"

As expected, Blessing's face softened into a silly sweetness. "Man, she's perfect. I never thought I'd meet someone like her, you know? Like, she really sees me and she cares about people and she makes amazing art. It's an incredible combination. She was at a protest the other day, and when she came back in, I swear she was buzzing—you could feel it on her skin. Like, she's got all this energy in her."

"She was at a protest? With the Assata kids?"

Blessing came back down to earth. "Don't start, Bitter."

"I eh say nothing!"

"You didn't have to say anything, that's how loud your thoughts are."

"I just want to know if she going to start dragging you with her to those things. I want you to stay safe, that's all."

"She wouldn't be dragging me—I can choose to walk there on my own, you know?"

"That's not what I meant."

Blessing swung her legs off her bed and stood up. "You gotta stop being so scared of Assata. They're not the dangerous ones in Lucille." She held out a hand to Bitter. "Come on, let's go down to lunch."

Bitter wanted to remind her that this was Lucille, everything and everyone was dangerous, but she swallowed the words and took Blessing's hand. Sometimes it was easier to just let things go. After all, at the end of the day, Bitter would still be able to go back to her room, lock the door, and draw something that was more real than anything they'd talked about. That was what mattered.

- - - -

It took the new boy about a week to ask Bitter out. He came up to her in the cafeteria during breakfast, while she was waiting at the omelet station, watching the onions and peppers sweat into the cook's pan.

"Hi," he said, standing in front of her. He was wearing too much denim—blue jeans and a denim shirt with a denim jacket over it. On anyone else, it would have looked corny as hell, but on him, it managed to look good. "Bitter, right?"

She balanced her tray on her hip. "Yes. And you're . . . Aloe?"

He grinned, flashing the gap in his front teeth. "Yes. I've been trying to run into you since that night we met, but you're always around people."

Bitter shrugged. "I like people."

Aloe's eyes were warm and amused. "Me, I'm more shy, but Alex helped me build my courage."

"Courage for what?"

"Ah." He ducked his head and looked up at her from under thick eyelashes, his locs falling over his face. "I wanted to ask if—if you'd go on a date with me?"

Bitter nearly dropped her tray in surprise, her glass of orange juice wobbling precariously. She steadied it against the omelet counter as the cook cracked two eggs into the pan and Aloe looked on with those eyes of his.

"A date? You don't think that's a little old-school?"

"I like old-school."

Bitter bit back a smile. Was this what Blessing had meant when she said he wasn't the hookup type? Bitter couldn't remember the last time anyone had asked her out like this, if ever. It was always, Oh, let's hang out, swing by my room, we'll watch a movie or something. "Okay," she said, because she couldn't think of a reason to say no.

Aloe grinned. "Let me collect your number," he said, his voice thrumming with pleasure. Bitter gave it to him and watched as he typed, his lashes dark against his cheeks. When he slid his phone back into his pocket, she watched the collar of his shirt slide to reveal a part of his collarbone. He would be fun to draw, she thought. "I'll text you," Aloe was saying, smiling as he walked backward, away from her. He waited until Bitter nodded before he raised a hand and turned around, dipping into the stream of students flowing between cafeteria tables. Barely two seconds later, Blessing popped up next to Bitter.

"Did he just get your number?" she asked, her voice squeaky with excitement. "Ooh, ooh, ooh! Are y'all gonna 'hang out'?" She waggled her eyebrows and giggled at the mock outrage on Bitter's face.

"He would have to work fuh that," Bitter replied with a smirk.

Blessing looked genuinely confused. "Since when?"

Bitter smacked her arm. "Shut up!" She smiled at the cook, thanking them as she took her plate of eggs, then headed with Blessing to their usual table, where Alex was soaking a stack of pancakes in an unholy amount of syrup.

Blessing stared at her girlfriend, aghast. "Baby!"

Alex looked up. "What?" A few bubbles dribbled out of the bottle as she squeezed the last of the syrup onto her plate. "This shit is delicious. Wet and delicious." She winked at Blessing. "Just how I like it." Blessing blushed as Alex reached out to grab a piece of bacon off her plate, dragging it through the puddle of syrup before popping it into her mouth.

Bitter slid her tray onto the table and sat down with them, glancing over as they bickered. Alex's eyes were always so soft when she looked at Blessing. Sometimes it was hard for Bitter to see their affection without feeling a little lonely herself. She tried to shake off the feeling. Maybe she would call up a little creature later, when she was alone in her room. The drawings could make her feel better, but they could also make her feel even more isolated, like there was a part of her life that she'd never be able to share with anyone because it was too strange, too different, and she had no idea how to explain it. Bitter had spent most of her life holding secrets, and she was good at it, but they could get real heavy, especially when you were carrying them alone.

"Whatchu gonna wear on your date?" Blessing asked, snapping Bitter back to the table.

Bitter shrugged. "The usual?"

Both Blessing and Alex looked at her outfit, the paint-splattered overalls and the worn sweatshirt underneath. "Absolutely the fuck not," Blessing said.

"I like it," Bitter replied, taking a bite of her eggs. "I eh dressing up for no guy."

"She has a point," Alex said, and Blessing rolled her eyes at both of them.

A wave of energy rippled around the cafeteria, and Bitter turned her head to see Miss Virtue walking through, dressed in a green snakeskin suit, her hair sculpted into an elaborate pompadour with a long braid down her back. She looked, as she always did, both formidable and like she wasn't really part of the rest of the world around her. Bitter slipped off her chair and darted between the tables until she was interrupting Miss Virtue's path.

"Sorry, pardon me, do you have a minute?"

Miss Virtue looked down at her, and Bitter felt the familiar shock of being in the woman's line of sight, those gray eyes piercing through Bitter's skin. "Yes, child?"

"I was wondering if I could make an appointment to talk about staying on at Eucalyptus. . . ."

Miss Virtue frowned. "You're only in your junior year."

Bitter set her jaw. "I like to plan ahead."

"Are you sure you want to stay at the school? You don't have to decide right now, you know."

A cold thread of fear wound around Bitter's spine. Was Miss Virtue trying to gently push her out into the world? The thought of not having Eucalyptus as a sanctuary was almost enough to tip her into a panic attack. Miss Virtue must have seen some of the alarm in her eyes, because she reached out and placed an elegant ringed hand on Bitter's shoulder.

"You will always be safe here," Miss Virtue said. "That doesn't mean that you can't be safe somewhere else too."

Bitter nodded, not trusting herself to speak. Miss Virtue looked at her kindly and brushed her fingertips against Bitter's cheek. "Come by my office this week," she said. "We'll talk more about it then." She drifted away, leaving touches of sandalwood and citron in the air behind her. Bitter headed back to her table, and Blessing raised an eyebrow at her.

"What was that all about?"

Bitter shrugged. "Nothing," she said. She knew her best friend wouldn't believe her, but also wouldn't push, and sure enough, Blessing and Alex fell right back into their banter. Bitter finished her breakfast, letting their voices wash over her and reminding herself that this was what home sounded like.

- - - -

For their date, Aloe took Bitter to a café a few blocks from the city center, within walking distance of Eucalyptus. "Alex told me you like the menu here," he said. "It's from the islands?"

Bitter smiled. "Yeah. Only place in Lucille where you could get doubles."

"Doubles?"

She laughed. "You'll like them. You could eat spicy food, right?"

Aloe pushed out his chest. "Ah, of course!"

"Good." The staff greeted Bitter warmly as they entered, and she put in their orders before leading Aloe to an overstuffed mustard-yellow sofa in the back of the shop. "This one of my favorite places outside the school."

He settled into a corner of the couch and looked around. "It's a nice place. I love that they have zobo on the menu."

Bitter giggled. "You mean sorrel?"

"Same difference."

They smiled at each other, and then the server brought over their food and drinks: several orders of doubles, an iced hibiscus for Aloe, and a double espresso for Bitter, who explained the different pepper levels in the doubles and watched as Aloe tasted them.

"These can't be vegetarian," he said, his mouth full and his eyes wide.

"Swear down," Bitter replied. "Is just fried dough and curry chana."

"I didn't know chickpeas could taste this good. Did your mother use to make this for you?" There was an awkward moment as Aloe, his face flushed with embarrassment, realized what he'd said. Kids didn't end up at Eucalyptus because they had good or even alive parents; it was tactless to pry into their old lives. "I'm sorry," he said, choking down his doubles. "I shouldn't have asked that."

"It's fine." Bitter gave a little smile. "We all find out sooner or later where we come from." She met his eyes, making sure her lost years were staying lost in her head even as she answered. "My mother died when I was a baby. I ended up in foster care."

"Like Alex."

Bitter nodded, even though she hadn't known that about Alex. "Like a lot of us. What about you?"

A shadow seeped into Aloe's eyes. "My parents kicked me out when I told them I was queer." He shrugged. "They said the usual—they didn't raise me to be like this, I wasn't welcome under their roof until I repented, rubbish like that."

"I'm sorry," Bitter said. "Blessing's parents were also like that. Said it was haram."

"Ah, she told me. Conversion therapy, even." He shook his head. "I'm glad she got out."

"I'm glad you got out too." Bitter wanted to reach out and touch his knee or something, but she felt too awkward to try. "How did Miss Virtue find you? One of the social workers?"

Aloe chuckled. "Actually, it's me that found her."

Bitter laughed in disbelief. "Yuh joking."

"I'm telling you. I met an Assata member who was recruiting, and they told me about Eucalyptus, so I came to find out for myself."

Bitter frowned. "Why didn't they recruit you for Assata? Why would they send you to Eucalyptus instead?"

Aloe sipped at his iced hibiscus, his brow furrowed. "I

wanted to make art. They thought it would be a good fit. Why wouldn't they have recommended Eucalyptus? They do it all the time."

Bitter didn't answer. She thought Assata looked down on Eucalyptus; the idea of one of them sending Aloe there instead of brainwashing him into their cause didn't make sense to her. Aloe glanced past her and broke out into a grin, waving a hand.

"Eddie!" he called. "Over here!"

Bitter turned, her stomach dropping. Eddie was at the counter in tiny denim shorts and a neon-pink crop top, her eyes outlined in matching pink eyeliner and her spiked purple braids pulled up in a ponytail. Bitter watched nervously as she strolled over to their couch.

"Hey, Aloe," she said, ignoring Bitter.

Aloe didn't pick up on any of the tension between the girls. "Hey, Eddie! This is my friend Bitter. Bitter, this is Eddie."

Eddie gave Bitter a scathing glance. "We've met," she said, her voice cold.

Aloe looked taken aback. "Ah. Is something wrong?"

"I mean . . ." Eddie examined her nails. "Other than the fact that she's lowkey trash. You sure this is who you wanna be spending your time with?"

"What the fuck did you just say?" Bitter stood up in one fluid, aggressive movement. "Yuh better watch your damn mouth before ah swell it up for yuh."

Eddie's snarl widened. "Bitch, I'd like to see you try."

Aloe jumped up. "That's enough!" He glanced between them, looking upset and confused. "What the hell? Why are you two even quarreling?"

Eddie tossed her braids. "Ask your *friend*," she said. "I'm out. Hit me up later, Aloe."

With one last glare at Bitter, she was gone, and Bitter was left with her hands clenched tightly into fists. She hadn't fought since before Eucalyptus, and the surge of blind furious adrenaline was both terribly familiar and uncomfortable. Aloe's gentle touch on her shoulder brought her back down, and she turned to meet his worried eyes.

"What was that?" he asked, keeping his voice soft. "Is everything okay?"

"It's fine," Bitter replied. "We just—we've bumped heads a few times, that's all."

"That was more than bumping heads. Were you two friends before or something?"

Bitter barked out a short laugh. "Friends? Never." She let Aloe pull her back down on the couch even though her spine was tense and her muscles were still humming with adrenaline.

"Here, relax," he said. "Take a deep breath and tell me about it."

Bitter held herself away from him, fighting the urge to

curl up on that mustard sofa and tell him everything, how it wasn't even about Eddie, it was about all the things underneath. She twisted her fingers together and looked down at her tangled hands. All these feelings were knotted inside her—how helpless she felt, how hopeless Lucille felt, how even talking about change felt like a joke, a cruel hope. Aloe was a stranger, and if there was one thing Bitter had learned, it was that you couldn't tell things to a stranger. But Aloe was still looking at her, curious and open, and Bitter found herself taking a deep breath after all. There was no point in having a home, in finally feeling safe at Eucalyptus, if she wasn't going to at least *try* to unravel some of these knots. And yes, Aloe was a stranger, but Bitter had also learned that some strangers could be kind. In that moment, she decided to trust him, because she was so, so tired of feeling this alone.

"I'm listening," he said. "Tell me what's wrong."

Bitter nodded. The words felt like she was chipping them off a frozen block before forcing them through her teeth. "Okay," she replied stiffly. "I'll try."

CHAPTER 3

Two hours later, Bitter and Aloe had run through what felt like half the café's supply of iced hibiscus tea. She had told him how Assata thought Eucalyptus kids didn't give a fuck about what was happening in Lucille and how pointless she thought all the protests were. "The mayor don't care, you know?" She broke a piece of fruitcake with her fingers, watching the raisins tumble to the plate. "Only thing that happens is more and more people keep getting hurt, keep dying. Someone said after the shoot-out last year, they didn't even return the bodies to their families. Just threw them into a grave together."

A spasm of pain crossed Aloe's face at that, but he watched her thoughtfully. "What do you think they should do?" he asked.

Bitter looked up. "Who?"

He shrugged. "Anyone. Everyone. Instead of fighting, what else should they do to change things?"

She laughed and looked away. He didn't want to hear the answer to that question. No one ever wanted to hear the answer to that question.

"I'm serious," he continued. "I want to know what you think."

Fine, then. "There eh nothing to do," Bitter snapped, her voice heavy. She didn't want to look at him. "Everyone does keep fighting and fighting, one generation after another, and nothing changes. If you born lucky, then you live lucky. Otherwise . . ." She let her voice trail off because it had nowhere to go. "It is what it is."

Saying the words made Bitter feel like a dark cloud had hugged her, wrapping her in soft, thick gray, numbing her skin. She pulled her knees up on the sofa and picked at the ring in her lip, circling it around. Aloe probably wasn't going to like her now, but that didn't matter. None of this mattered; none of this was real. Her little spiral was interrupted by the sound of Aloe chuckling softly to himself.

Bitter glared at him. "What's so funny?" If he was laughing at her, she was going to punch him in the face.

Aloe leaned forward and took her hand, the warmth of his palm surprising her. His eyes were gentle. "No, no, nothing is funny," he said, even as he smiled. "I just—I don't believe you."

"Excuse me?"

He squeezed her hand, and a small thrill rushed over Bitter's skin. She ignored it, holding her breath as Aloe kept talking, his words tripping over each other in their animation.

"I don't believe that you think nothing can change. You're an artist! You imagine things all the time, and you're trying to tell me that you can't imagine anything different from this? Another kind of world? That you've *never* imagined something better than what's happening now?"

Bitter exhaled softly and pulled her hand away. Another world. She bit the inside of her lip as a traitorous memory crept up on her, smelling like ash and blood and salt. There had been one photograph. One photograph of the woman who shared Bitter's hard cheekbones and bare eyebrows, the same wide mouth. Her mother, trapped in an image forever, before she'd met the monster that would make her daughter, before Bitter was ever born. Her last guardians had given it to Bitter when she was much younger, in a rare moment of kindness. "So at least yuh could know what she looked like," the woman had said. "Since you can't remember."

Well, Bitter would never forget, not after she drew her mother over and over again, forming the lines of her face until they were perfect, her tall figure with the graceful dress. She'd practiced until it was flawless, then Bitter had cut herself to wake the drawing up, dabbing her blood on her mother's face, on her sleeves, her neck, her hands. She tried it so many times, until people started noticing her cut-up arms and the woman she lived with pulled her aside and warned her to stop whatever nonsense she was doing because they weren't doing anything to her and she was walking around making them look bad. Bitter kept trying, hid the cuts better, but one day as she was sobbing over a splattered drawing, she realized it was never going to work. Her mother was never going to come back to life, and that was never going to change. That was never going to be different.

She had burned the photograph then. It wasn't real and it didn't matter. Her mother's face met her every morning in the mirror, and besides, Bitter's muscles couldn't forget how to draw her even if she tried to wash the memory away. Aloe was staring at her.

"Don't you imagine something better?" he was asking. "Ever?"

Bitter stared back at him. "I used to," she said. "I stopped."

"Why?" His voice was urgent, his face sharpened into intensity. "You live in Eucalyptus. I'm sure that's better than wherever you came from. Things *changed* for you, Bitter. They changed for me. The fact that we're sitting here proves it. Why can't you believe that they can change for Lucille too?"

"Why's it so important to you?" she shot back. "What I believe, what I doh believe. You recruiting for Assata now, or what?"

"No, I just—"

"Allyuh does like to say the same damn thing over and over. *Change, believe, something better.* What if there's nothing better? What if you keep feeding people this—this *hope* that eh going nowhere!"

Aloe took her hand again, grabbing it so hard that the bones pressed against each other. "Hope is what we *need,*" he said. "Hope is what got me out of my father's house, what helped me keep going. Don't you want to keep going?"

Tears built behind Bitter's eyes, flooding her head. "No," she whispered, shocked to hear the truth leave her mouth. "No, I want to stop. I want it to stop, I want everything to stop." She was crying now, and this was why she didn't like to talk about these things, why she walked away and drew something real instead, because now that she'd started, she couldn't make herself stop any more than she could make the world stop. "It hurting all the time and I cyah feel it, I cyah let mehself feel it, 'cause then ah go break in so many pieces, yuh could never find enough of me to put back together. How yuh expect me to go fight, be out there facing these people who doh care if we alive or if we dead, they killing us all the time and is ah game to them. All we doing is throwing more and more of us into their damn teeth. Fuh what? Fuh *hope?*"

She sniffled and dragged the sleeve of her sweatshirt across her face, swiping roughly at her eyes and nose. Aloe had let go of her hand, but he was still listening intently, his eyes soft.

"Hope is a waste of fucking time," Bitter said. "It doh matter if we at the school—you know how many kids they never find? How many girls like me just . . . disappear because someone selling them? Is like we get a life jacket and then you still know there's people out there drowning and you just sitting on a boat watching them drown and you remember what the drowning was like but you cyah bring yourself to go back." She shook her head. "It doh matter. We cyah make all of us safe, and unless all of us are safe, none of us are safe."

Bitter grabbed a napkin and blew her nose loudly, not caring how she looked in front of Aloe anymore. He probably couldn't even understand half of what she was saying, she had slipped so strongly back into her accent. This date was already a disaster. She just wanted to go back to Eucalyptus, put on her headphones, and lie in bed listening to something loud enough to erase all these feelings she'd thrown up in front of this guy.

"Hey." Aloe touched her wrist lightly, and Bitter looked up to see him staring at her, his own eyes damp. "Can I give you a hug?" he asked, his voice tentative. "Please?"

She was so surprised that he was crying, all she could do was nod, and then Aloe was wrapping his arms around her, swallowing her up in his wingspan, in his broad shoulders and chest, anchoring her. Bitter felt her heart wrench—he was hugging her like he needed to be held too, so she slid her arms around his ribs, smelling the lemon of his shirt, his back wide under her hands. Tension clicked free inside her, loosening her muscles, and she let out a jagged breath against his neck.

"You're not alone," Aloe whispered. "I know how impossible it feels. I know it hurts. You don't have to feel any of this alone, Bitter." He released her, and Bitter wiped at her eyes again, not sure if she could believe him. "And hope is not a waste of time. Hope is a *discipline.*" Aloe said the words with such complete confidence, with such a backbone of faith, that this time Bitter let them seep into her, just enough to register. She knew about discipline from her work; she knew about rigor and how you had to practice and practice and practice until you carried it with you in your bones. She'd never thought of hope like that—as something serious and deliberate instead of something wishful and desperate.

"Where did you learn that?" she asked. The words had sounded too old for his mouth.

Aloe broke into a grin. "Mariame Kaba," he said. "An organizer who fights for prisons to be abolished. Assata taught it to me—she's been one of their Elders for a while now."

Bitter filed the information away in her head, but she frowned when he mentioned Assata. "How do you know Eddie?" she asked. "How did you two even meet?" She tried not to feel some kind of way about how Aloe's face lit up at the question.

"I'm training to be a protest medic," he said, his voice tinged with pride in his work. "Eddie connected me to the trainers at Assata."

Bitter blinked, taken aback. "I thought you were a sound artist?"

"Yes, but it's also so powerful as a tool for healing. I started doing healing circles with organizers and protesters—that's how I met Eddie—and then I thought maybe I could help in a more immediate way, you know?"

"Wow. That's . . . amazing." Bitter felt a little awkward. Imagining Aloe in a circle trying to help other people was such a gentle image that it reminded her how Assata technically did more than just protest. Alex had been telling her and Blessing about their food program once, but Bitter had tuned out like she always did. She felt a little guilty about it now.

Aloe checked his phone and whistled. "We're about to miss dinner—we've been here for hours." He grinned at her. "But I think we can make it back in time if we walk fast. Today's roasted breadfruit—I begged the chef for it. Blessing said it's one of your favorites, and this café only makes it once in a while?"

Bitter blushed hard. "You asked them to make it? For me?"

Aloe stood up and reached out his hand. "Of course. I wanted today to be the perfect date." His eyes crinkled with pleasure. "And it really was." Bitter just sat there, staring at him, and Aloe laughed, grabbing her hand impatiently. "Come on!" he said.

When Aloe pulled her off the sofa, Bitter stumbled as she stood up, catching herself against his chest. Time staggered to a halt as she realized that his face was now just a breath away from hers. The air thickened into honey, and Bitter looked up into Aloe's eyes, flecks of light reflected in the soft brown. His face had shifted, his pupils dilating as he reached up a hand and brushed his fingers along Bitter's jaw, sending rippling goose bumps over her skin.

"You are so beautiful," he said, his gaze bathing her face like light. "Is it okay if I kiss you?"

Bitter couldn't quite speak—there wasn't enough oxygen

somehow—but she managed a nod, and Aloe flashed a crooked grin as he leaned in, sliding his hand to the back of her head. His lips brushed against Bitter's, and every nerve in her body was instantly scalded with heat singing loudly through her. She wrapped her arms around his neck and kissed him back, not caring that everyone in the café could see them, because in that moment, it felt like anything was possible, even another world.

CHAPTER 4

A few days later, Bitter sat in Miss Virtue's office, waiting for her to return from a meeting with the Eucalyptus chef. Miss Virtue's redhead secretary had waved her in without even glancing up, so Bitter had a chance to look around without Miss Virtue's imposing presence filling up all the air. She wanted to see what new art Miss Virtue had put up—the principal treated her office a little bit like a gallery, rotating artwork in and out every month. Since the office was mostly glass (as if Miss Virtue couldn't quite stand to have walls around her), a lot of the art she displayed there were freestanding pieces that only needed air and space. Soft patterned rugs were layered over the floor, and the chairs and desk were carved antiques in a deep walnut. Bitter didn't like to look too closely at the carvings. They seemed to shift into terrifying shapes the longer one stared at them. Instead, she fixed her eyes on a sculpture she hadn't seen before, installed in a corner of the room. The base of the piece was a white-washed cinder block, extending into carved wood and culminating in a dark horn that spiked toward the ceiling. Bitter was tracing the curves of the wood with her eyes when Miss Virtue's voice startled her.

"Do you like that piece?"

Bitter spun around, rising up out of the chair. "Yes!" she blurted out. "I think so."

Miss Virtue closed the office door behind her. She was wearing a blood-red dress with severe lines, and her silver hair was pulled away from her face, cinched into a tight bun at the nape of her neck. Her lips were a deeper red than her dress, and when she smiled at Bitter, her teeth seemed almost sharp.

"That's Jack Whitten's *Lichnos*," she said. "You learned about him in your art history class, I believe?"

Bitter nodded, glancing back at the sculpture. "I didn't know any of his work was here at the school. I thought they all in the museums."

Miss Virtue walked around her desk, gesturing for Bitter to sit back down. "Most of them, yes." A brief gleam entered her gray eyes. "I have a few . . . connects."

No part of Bitter wanted to ask any follow-up questions. As respectable as Miss Virtue looked, there was always that simmering energy in her, smelling faintly of menace and a shadowed past. It would have been disturbing if Bitter hadn't always been sure that Miss Virtue was on the side of the Eucalyptus kids. She did feel sorry for whoever fell on her *bad* side, though.

"So," Miss Virtue said, sitting and crossing her legs at the knee. "You're worried about after graduation. You still have over a year, you know?"

Bitter fidgeted in her chair. "Yes, Miss, but I does like to plan ahead." There had been too many years when she'd had no control over her future, and the thought of leaving it vague and unresolved made her stomach churn.

The corners of Miss Virtue's mouth turned up a little. "That's smart. A lot of the students would wait until their last term to think about this."

Bitter made a face. "That doh make no sense."

This time Miss Virtue laughed out loud. It should have been a reassuring sound, but again there was something about her teeth that sent a frisson of wariness down Bitter's spine. *She's dangerous,* her instincts whispered, *just not to you.*

"So, you would like to stay on at the school."

Bitter decided to be halfway honest. "I doh see a lot of other options. It not like being an artist does pay the bills."

Miss Virtue raised an eyebrow. "You do know we give out those graduation grants to get you started, yes? You met

Eucalyptus artists with perfectly sustainable careers when we did studio visits last term."

"Yeah, but they're . . ." Bitter's voice trailed into silence. *Good,* she'd meant to say. *They're good at what they do.* She couldn't quite voice it to Miss Virtue, though, not when the woman believed in her students with a faith that could set fire to water. Bitter didn't want to admit that she didn't think she'd be able to make it on her own, even with the starter money Eucalyptus provided, sourced from no one knew where because no one had the nerve to ask Miss Virtue how the hell the school could afford a fraction of the things it provided the kids.

The silence in the office sat for a few minutes, clouded in the air, as Miss Virtue made no attempt to prompt Bitter for the rest of her sentence, and Bitter just stared down at her paint-splattered sneakers. Sunlight poured through the glass walls, and Bitter could hear the wind whistling in the trees outside. She took a deep breath and let it fill the bottoms of her lungs.

"I doh want to live out there," she said, her voice low. "It's not safe." She raised her eyes to Miss Virtue's. "You *know* it's not safe." The woman had to know. She was the one who had rescued them from the things out there.

Miss Virtue nodded. Her lashes were dark and spiked, and she blinked so infrequently that it was unnerving to maintain eye contact with her for any length of time. "You want to stay where it's safe."

She said it in a matter-of-fact way, but Bitter bristled at the words. "I'm not a coward," she snapped. "Being out there doh make anyone braver than anyone else." In Bitter's opinion, all it meant was that you were reckless and possibly a bit dotish.

Miss Virtue raised a narrow hand, and Bitter bit her tongue, falling back in her seat and folding her arms across her chest, waiting for the scolding to come.

It didn't.

"You are allowed to feel safe," Miss Virtue said. Bitter blinked, and tears heated her eyes because the words were so simple, yet so heavy with permission. The principal's voice was as kind as when she'd first welcomed Bitter to Eucalyptus, when she'd told her that people didn't know a school could be a forever home, but that Eucalyptus was special, just like Bitter.

Miss Virtue narrowed her eyes, as if she'd just seen into Bitter's memory. "When we say forever, we mean it, you know?"

Bitter felt a tear spill down her cheek at that, but she swiped it away with her sleeve. "I know," she said, her voice thick.

Miss Virtue looked thoughtful. "I'm not sure you do."

She steepled her fingers together and leaned her elbows on the desk. "This will always be your home, but I would be remiss if I didn't encourage my students to go out into the world as well. We provide safety here, or at least we try our very best to, but safety is also something you can *make* for yourself, Bitter, even if it doesn't feel like it now."

Bitter wasn't sure she agreed. She would have made herself safe so many times before if she could have. She had *tried*. It hadn't worked.

"It not that easy," she managed to say. She was not going to cry in front of Miss Virtue—she'd done it too many times before. "You need other things to be safe, and Lucille doh have them—it just have the opposite."

Miss Virtue made a small sound in her throat. "Lucille is certainly . . . chaotic."

That was one way to put it, Bitter thought. It's not how she would've described a city that was also a crisis, but whatever.

"You can build safety in community, however," Miss Virtue continued. "The bonds you have with the other students here, do you feel safe within them?"

Bitter didn't even have to think. "Of course."

"Then that's a start." Miss Virtue glanced at her watch. "I have another meeting, but the answer to your question is yes, Bitter. You may stay on at Eucalyptus as long as you need. Leaving will always be your choice, and your choice alone."

"But one day I *will* choose to leave, is what you saying."

Miss Virtue's head tilted to the side, and her eyes softened a bit. "Everyone does, eventually. When they're ready."

The office door opened and the secretary poked her head in, her red curls tight to her scalp and her glasses reflecting the sunlight. "Come along," she said to Bitter. "Your boyfriend's been waiting for you."

Bitter blushed, and Miss Virtue gave her a playful look. "Oh, you got a boyfriend now, huh?"

"No, he's . . . we're . . ." Bitter gave up and grabbed her backpack. "Thanks for the talk, Miss Virtue!"

The principal chuckled and pulled out her phone. "You're welcome, child."

Bitter made her way past the secretary's amused look, and sure enough, Aloe was sitting in the waiting area, holding a small gift bag on his knees. He raised his head as Bitter emerged from the office, and his face broke into a huge smile. It made blood rush to Bitter's face, how openly Aloe showed his pleasure at her presence. Sometimes she wondered how he found the courage to flash emotions as if no one could hurt him with them. He unfolded from his seat and held out his arms for a hug.

"Hey, gorgeous," he said.

Bitter felt the secretary's eyes on them, and so the hug she gave Aloe was awkward and hurried. He didn't seem to mind, chattering on as they left the office.

"I have a surprise for you," he said, and Bitter couldn't help but smile at how excited he was.

"Is that what's in the bag?" she asked.

Aloe faked shock. "How did you know?" He handed her the gift bag as they walked down a brick path that led to the photography studios, where Bitter was meeting Blessing for a portrait session. Aloe had drum circle in a few minutes, but he'd insisted on walking Bitter from Miss Virtue's office to Blessing's studio just so he could steal a little more time with her. Bitter tried to focus on how romantic it was so that she wouldn't start to freak out about how this much affection made her almost suspicious, like there would be something ugly coming right after it. The gift bag wasn't helping. There was no reason for him to get her a present—it was random and uncalled for, and for an uncharitable moment, Bitter wondered what Aloe was trying to get from her. The gold foil of the bag reflected sunlight into her eyes as she pulled out thin sheets of decorative green paper. Nestled underneath was a clear box filled with small, crystallized spheres in a sticky brown that washed all of Bitter's prickly feelings away, replacing them with a sweetness that stung.

"Where you find tamarind balls?" Her voice pitched high

with excitement as she popped the box open and immediately threw one into her mouth. It was a childhood taste that burst on her tongue, a fleeting memory of a time before the terrible times, a taste she had almost forgotten existed, and Bitter dragged in a deep breath edged in sugar as Aloe laughed.

"I put in some work," he said. "You mentioned them once, and I thought maybe you'd like to taste them again."

Bitter stared at him for a moment. He had no idea, she thought, truly no idea, how much of someone's world he could shift just by being himself. "Thank you," she said, because all the other things wouldn't fit in her mouth. They had come up to Blessing's studio, and the bell for the next hour was ringing. "You going to be late for circle."

Aloe grinned and kissed her cheek. "Worth it," he said, then waved and jogged off. Bitter watched him leave, staring, the box of sweetness in her hand and the gold bag dangling from her fingers. A chuckle interrupted her, and she whipped her head around to see Blessing smirking in the doorway of the studio.

"Checking out your man, huh?"

Bitter blushed and pushed past her best friend. "Doh start with me." She put the tamarind balls carefully back into the gift bag, but Blessing snatched it away from her.

"Ooh, what's this?"

Bitter made a half-hearted attempt to snatch it back. "None of your damn business."

"He's a keeper if he buying you gifts," Blessing noted as she lifted the lid of the box and sniffed at the tamarind balls. "These smell good!"

"You can't have any."

"Girl, I don't want your love candies." She winked at Bitter and put the bag on a table. "Is this what you're wearing for your portrait?"

Bitter glanced down at her pinstriped overalls and her paint-splattered sweater. "Yeah. Is that a problem? You said to dress like I would normally dress. I was supposed to change clothes?"

Blessing waved a hand and shook her head. "Nah, you good. You look like yourself. That's what we want." She had already set up the backdrop they'd designed together earlier that week, a terra-cotta sheet that Bitter had painted with liberal streaks of green and pink accented by a few touches of white. Blessing stepped behind her camera to adjust the lens, gesturing for Bitter to take her position, and a familiar warmth spread through Bitter's chest.

When she'd first come to Eucalyptus, she hadn't looked or felt like herself. In fact, she couldn't have told anyone what that even meant. The man and woman who had housed her insisted that she wear her hair straight, and even when Bitter refused to relax it, they made her iron it until every curl was flat and dead. She tried to coax the curls back when she moved into Eucalyptus, but they were as hurt as her heart—wilted and folded—and so Bitter had ended up sobbing in front of a bathroom mirror and hacking away at her damaged hair with a pair of blunt scissors she'd borrowed from the reception desk. Blessing had walked in then, all holographic stickers and flawless eyeliner, and the two girls had stared at each other for a few seconds before Blessing said, "I can shave it off for you if you want." As if it was no big deal. As if it wasn't years of bad life caught up in there. Bitter hadn't even trusted herself to speak, so she'd just nodded, and Blessing had burst into animated movement, and within an hour, Bitter was looking at someone new in her reflection, curls cut low to her head, her cheekbones high and proud.

"I gotta take a picture of you," Blessing had said, darting out of the room and returning with her camera. That was the first portrait they'd made together, and it was one of the first times Bitter could look at an image of herself and feel like she wasn't looking at a stranger formed by someone else's hands. The two girls made it into a tradition, and now Bitter stood in Blessing's studio surrounded by the images her best friend had made. Blessing had a gift for excavating a person's spirit until it shone through their face and could be seized in her camera.

Bitter tugged at the neck of her sweater. "You sure you don't want me in some earrings or something?" she asked.

Blessing rolled her eyes. "Since when do you wear earrings?"

"I does wear them sometimes!"

"Yeah, sure." Blessing grinned at her. "Your makeup looks great—don't even worry about jewelry. Plus, you already have your lip ring in." She passed over a paintbrush tipped in yellow. "Just hold this up, please."

"Really?" Bitter's voice was colored in skepticism. "A painter holding a paintbrush?"

Blessing shot her a stern look. "Yes. You got a problem with holding a tool of your trade?"

Bitter shrugged. "It a little obvious, you don't think?"

"Chile, you walk around *literally* covered in paint," Blessing retorted. "I think we're well past the point of obvious. Raise your arm some more."

Bitter held back a retort and kept quiet as Blessing directed her for the next several shots. Her best friend wasn't wrong—it was just that Bitter felt a little silly if she thought too hard about identifying as a painter. No one had told her until Eucalyptus that it was something she could do seriously, and Blessing was one of the loudest voices insisting that Bitter was a real artist, forcing her to hold a brush and stare into a camera and, for those minutes, not pretend she was something different or someone less. Would she be able to hold on to herself if she left the school and went back out into the world? Miss Virtue had made it sound like it was possible to build a safe place anywhere, as long as you had the right people, but Bitter wasn't quite sure she believed that.

Blessing lifted up her camera and stepped around to show Bitter some of the shots. "You look amazing, sis," she said, her voice gentle as she tilted the screen.

Bitter stared down, and her mouth curved into a small smile. There she was. Brush held up like a flag, eyes staring forward like there was nothing to be afraid of behind her, looking like *herself.*

A wave of gratitude flooded her, for everything: for Miss Virtue reminding her that this was a forever home, for Aloe and sweet little things he brought with his hands, for Blessing and the way she made sure Bitter remembered herself.

"Thank you," she whispered, so softly that she wasn't sure her friend could hear her, but then Blessing wrapped her arms tightly around Bitter and squeezed hard.

"I got you," Blessing said, as if she could tell that Bitter had been scared, as if she wanted to drown out the fear. Bitter took a deep breath and hugged her best friend back, knowing that no matter what happened, at least she could count on being safe in Blessing's eyes.

CHAPTER 5

A week later, Bitter was pacing nervously in her room, watching the time slip past on her nightstand clock.

"Cyah believe I agree to this," she grumbled to herself, worry fluttering in her stomach.

She desperately wanted to draw one of her little creatures, just so she could feel grounded, but she only had a few minutes before Aloe showed up with Eddie. He'd insisted on mediating a conversation between them—the peacemaker in him couldn't sit still with two people he cared about hating each other that much. In the short time since their first date, Aloe had slipped into Bitter's life so seamlessly, so easily, that it was terrifying for Bitter, who felt like she could barely remember a time when Aloe wasn't there. Blessing and Alex loved him because although he was gentle, he wasn't afraid to argue with Bitter. He pushed where anyone else would have stepped back, and inch by reluctant inch, Bitter found herself stretching into someone she didn't quite know she could be.

She didn't get as defensive when debating with her friends, and she was learning how to stay and talk things through instead of shutting down and withdrawing. Aloe saw the world with such expansiveness that it widened her own field of vision. It softened her armor just seeing how soft he was. That was why she'd told him the truth about her and Eddie, after he kept asking why they got on each other's nerves so much. Aloe wasn't someone who deserved to be kept in the dark, but that didn't make telling him the truth any easier.

"We hooked up, okay?" Bitter had finally yelled after he brought it up for what felt like the thousandth time. "God, you does keep asking and asking!" She pulled anger around her like a warm and spiky blanket. Eddie was his friend—he was probably going to take her side. "We hooked up and I ghosted her because she doh ever stop talking about the damn revolution, looking at me like I eh doing enough to change the world. I not into all that! I just want peace and quiet." Bitter had slumped down on Aloe's bed, keeping her head low because she didn't want to meet his eyes. "Now yuh know. I was an asshole. Happy now?"

Aloe had sat next to her and taken her hand, a gesture she was recognizing as his way of reminding her that he was still there, that they were still connected. "It's no problem," he said, bending his head so he could meet her eyes, then giving her a warm grin. "I still like you."

Bitter snorted. "Even after how I treated your friend?"

Aloe shrugged. "Me, I've done things I'm not proud of. I definitely owe a few people some apologies."

"For true? What was the worst thing you did?"

Aloe winced. "I cheated on this guy."

"Mm, I've been there."

"With his sister."

Bitter choked back a laugh. "Okay, I haven't been there! Did he find out?"

"Oh yes." Aloe looked embarrassed. "Walked in on us. She didn't even know I was dating him."

This time Bitter couldn't hold back her giggles. "I'm sorry, that's terrible!"

"Laugh at my pain—it's fine." Aloe winked at her. "All I'm saying is, it's not too late to fix things with Eddie. I think both of you are so special, I want you to see each other better."

Bitter shook her head. "You really does want world peace and for everyone to get along."

Aloe leaned in and kissed her gently. "Yes," he said, his voice confident. "And that's why you like me." They'd tumbled back into his bed, and Bitter had honestly thought the conversation was over. A couple of days passed, and she was sketching in the Eucalyptus garden, listening while Aloe was playing around on a guitar.

"Eddie's coming by tomorrow," he'd said casually, as if it

was nothing. "I figured we could show her some of your art and then sit down and talk. What do you think?" He looked up at her, all helpful and innocent and well meaning, and although Bitter really wanted to cuss him out for making plans without her, she also knew it meant a lot to him for her to at least try with Eddie, so she just smiled tightly instead and said it was fine. He knew she would've said no if he asked, and it was just like him to count on her forgiving him rather than asking her for permission. For someone so sweet, Aloe could be equally sneaky.

Now Bitter was pacing in her room, tugging on her bedspread to smooth it out because the idea of Eddie seeing her space in any state other than controlled and perfect was more than she could stand.

"Why can't we meet somewhere neutral?" she'd complained to Aloe.

"Why can't you paint in a studio like everyone else?" he'd shot back.

"My room *is* my studio."

"Exactly. You're lucky Miss Virtue was nice enough to even give you that much space. I mean, we can go somewhere else, if you want to carry your work over there as well."

"I doh understand why I have to show her my work," Bitter grouched. "You very annoying with your peacemaker business."

"It's the best way for her to see what you're really about," Aloe had replied.

"Yeh? And what she going to show me in return?"

He'd gone serious then, looking at her with those eyes of his. "From what I know of what went down, I'd say her heart, if you're lucky," he'd said, and if anyone else had said that, it would have been corny as hell, but Aloe was so damn earnest that Bitter had no comeback. Although he wasn't judging, he seemed to know as well as she did that this whole matter rested on Eddie extending some grace that Bitter herself wasn't sure she deserved.

She still had a memory of the last time she'd been alone with Eddie, off campus at Eddie's parents' house. They were out at work and Eddie had snuck Bitter upstairs, where they'd spent the afternoon making out and playing around in her bed, clothes dropping off in degrees, laughing the way they did when they weren't fighting over how they chose to move through the world.

Afterwards, Bitter had slid out of bed while Eddie was sleeping and grabbed her clothes from the floor, a dull weight in her chest. It had seemed like the perfect moment to leave, in the gentle light of an afterglow, before it all inevitably went to shit. She'd given Eddie one last look before she tiptoed out of the door, and that last image had been seared onto the back of her eyes—Eddie sprawled out on lavender sheets, her braids sea green with gold cowries at the tips, her lips parted in her sleep. Bitter never called her again and never told her why she'd left like that. She hadn't told Aloe either. It stayed inside her, deliberately lost, and even though Aloe had the best intentions, Bitter was terrified of what this conversation was going to bring up. It had been so much easier to let Eddie hate her.

"Bitter? We're here!" Aloe's voice came cheerfully through the door as he knocked and pushed it open. Bitter spun around, her heart pounding in her chest. She'd never let Eddie come on campus back then. It was bad enough she was messing around with an Assata kid—she didn't need the rest of the school to know. Which meant Eddie had never seen her room, never stepped into her world, and now Aloe was waltzing her in here as if it was nothing. Bitter shoved her hands into the pockets of her overalls and tried to look nonchalant. Eddie came in behind Aloe, wearing a bright yellow romper, her braids twisted up into two large buns. She looked around Bitter's room: the large windows, the easels and drop cloths, Bitter's bed in a corner with an excessive number of pillows on it, the gray armchair pushed to the wall.

"Nice place," Eddie said politely, her eyes hidden behind round sunglasses. Aloe reached out and snatched the glasses off her face, holding them out of reach when Eddie lunged to get them back.

"Come on," he said. "You said you'd try."

The scab had fallen off the cut on Eddie's eyebrow, but there was a scar there, and it made Bitter uncomfortable, reminding her too much of what being on the front lines meant.

"Fine," Eddie snapped, glaring at Aloe, then swinging her gaze over to Bitter. "Look, your boy wants us to kiss and make up or whatever."

"That is *not* what I said!" Aloe protested.

"Whatever, Aloe." Eddie shrugged and gave Bitter a challenging look. "So now what? You gon' apologize for ghosting me or what?"

Embarrassment washed over Bitter in a hot wave. She hadn't been expecting Eddie to get so direct so quickly, especially with Aloe there. "It was complicated," she started to say, but Eddie kissed her teeth and held her hand out to Aloe.

"That's bullshit. Give me my glasses back, man. I'm out."

"*Eddie.* You said you'd try." Aloe's voice was calm, and it seemed to irritate Eddie as much as it did Bitter sometimes.

"I *am* trying! Your girl, on the other hand—"

Bitter couldn't resist snapping at her. "I have a name, you know."

Eddie stopped short, about three seconds away from losing her temper, and Aloe stepped in between them quickly.

"Okay, wait," he said. "Bitter, do you agree that you owe Eddie an apology?"

It was a sour idea to her—none of this was supposed to have gotten this far. What happened to the good old days when you could just ghost in peace and the other person got the message and there weren't any hurt feelings to have to clean up later? She huffed out a breath.

"Is possible," she admitted, then flinched as Eddie took a furious step toward her.

"It's possible? We dated for weeks; then you randomly snuck out of my room for no reason and ignored all my calls and texts without telling me anything! What the hell, Bitter?"

It did sound bad when Eddie laid it out like that, and Bitter didn't dare look over to see Aloe's reaction. This wasn't a version of herself she wanted him to meet. Aloe was deliberately tender, so focused on healing, and it made Bitter want to soften her sharp edges so she wouldn't cut him like she'd cut other people. He smelled like possibility, and it felt delicate, something to cup your hands around, something to protect from a harsh wind. She ran a hand over her scalp and turned to him.

"Let me talk to Eddie alone," Bitter said. Aloe blinked in surprise, then nodded, his face settling into its usual ease.

"No problem," he said. "Come and find me in the garden after?"

"Sure." Bitter felt a little bad about sending him away, but she wasn't the same person with Eddie as she was with him. For now, it seemed better to keep it separate. Aloe touched Eddie's arm on his way out and closed the door behind him.

Bitter took a deep breath and faced Eddie. "I'm sorry," she said. "For how I treated you, how I just . . . left."

Eddie looked surprised by the apology. "Really?"

"Yeh. I just—" Bitter paused and pulled together her courage. "I got scared. So I ran."

"Scared of what?"

It was much harder to be open with Eddie than with Aloe, but Bitter figured it was good practice. She met Eddie's eyes and tried to be someone better than she already was. "I was scared of you," she admitted. "Scared you think less of me because I'm not on the front lines like you. Like, maybe it was cute for us to hook up a few times, but at some point you'd look at me and resent me for not being more like you."

Eddie frowned. "I'm sorry if I said anything that made you feel that way. Why didn't you say something?"

"It just seemed easier not to. Like, there was so much shit—you could resent me, you could get hurt, and I just . . . I doh want to be close to all that shit out there. I'm sorry, I just doh want that to be my life."

68

"Right." Eddie folded her hands, and Bitter could tell she was a little offended but was holding it in. "No one was asking you to be out there with us, you know? That's not the point."

Bitter raised an eyebrow. "Really? Because it does feel like if everyone's not out there like Assata, then they not doing enough."

"Maybe that's just your own insecurity showing," Eddie retorted.

"You just said that to me the other day in the street!"

"I was pissed! For a good reason—you were a fucking asshole."

"Assata trash-talks Eucalyptus all the time. Doh act like it was just that once."

"And y'all talk shit too! But at the end of the day, who's sitting inside these nice walls and who's out there getting teargassed, Bitter? It's not the fucking same!"

"No one asked you to go get fucking gassed!"

"Wow." A betrayed hurt crept into Eddie's eyes. "For real, B?"

Fuck. Bitter sighed and took a step toward Eddie, but Eddie backed away. "I'm so sorry," Bitter said. "I eh mean it like that."

Eddie's jaw was set. "You know what I wanna know? What the fuck do *you* believe? Because I think I'm pretty clear about who I am and what I'm fighting for. Who the fuck are *you*?"

It was an excellent question. The best question, in fact. Bitter knew she had spent a long time hiding what she actually believed from people, and it was a hard habit to break, even when someone was looking at her with the amount of hurt Eddie had in her eyes. Only Blessing and now Aloe knew the truth about how Bitter did want a better world, but also about how hope had been beaten out of her, how it was safer to curl up in the pessimistic dark because then none of the horrific things would hurt as much because you'd made part of yourself dead to them, dead to anything else. Bitter knew that neither of them wanted her to live in that dark place, but Blessing was careful. She wasn't the type to barge in and shine a light in places someone had curled over to hide. Aloe was the opposite. He barged in, bulldozing his hope and belief into dusty corners, shaking out the rugs and asking questions about what was underneath. He was clumsy and gentle, annoying and soothing at the same time.

Bitter didn't want to turn into someone who kept talking about her fear. Fear was fine, but showing it made you weak. She'd learned that in the lost years, when hungry eyes watched her for what she was scared of so they could use it against her, and Bitter had learned it was better to be stoic, to be a blank and unfeeling wall, because if you were entirely armor and no underbelly, then they couldn't stab you in the soft places. She made a mental note to ask Aloe how he managed to move through the world with that tenderness, what kind of armor it gave him. Who were you? The armor or the person underneath? Was it possible for the two to fuse into one, and if so, how did you describe it to the girl standing in front of you, waiting for an answer?

"I don't have hope," Bitter found herself saying. "I don't know how allyuh does it, just go and keep putting yourselves out there. The police keep killing us and you does get all up in their faces like they can't kill you too. It eh make no sense. This been going on for years—what makes you think you can stop it? Don't you want to live?"

Eddie's face softened as she listened, realization dawning. "Oh, B. You're *scared*."

She said it so gently that Bitter had to bite down on her cheek to stop from bursting into tears. "Yuh think I'm a coward," she said, her heart sinking.

"No!" Eddie took a stride forward and grabbed Bitter's shoulders. "B, you're not a coward."

"If I wasn't scared, I go be out there with y'all, right?"

"B, listen to me." Eddie shook her slightly. "You don't have to have hope. You don't have to be out there. You're important just as you are. You matter."

Bitter couldn't hold back the tears then. It had been nice

to stay in the bubble of Eucalyptus with Aloe and Blessing, fenced in by Miss Virtue's assurance that she didn't have to leave, but Eddie was from the outside world, waist-deep in it, and Bitter couldn't look at her and pretend that everything was okay. Nothing was okay. "I'm not *doing* anything!" she sobbed, not resisting as Eddie pulled her into a tight hug. "I cyah stop any of it—no one can, or it would've been stopped by now. What's the point?"

"It's okay," Eddie whispered against her head. "You don't have to be one of us, Bitter. That's not how any revolution works. Everyone has their place—mine just happens to be out there. Yours is somewhere else." She glanced around Bitter's room. "In here, by the looks of it. Making your work. We need the artists too, you know?"

Bitter drew her head back. "Really?" It was the last thing she'd expected someone from Assata to say about someone from Eucalyptus.

Eddie rolled her eyes. "Girl, we *been* knowing that everyone got their own role. Whatchu think the Elders teach us? The revolution needs artists, just like it needs healers and storytellers, just like it needs the organizers and protesters. It's all one big organism working together."

"Then why you does give us so much shit?!"

Eddie made a face. "Well, it gets under our skin sometimes, you know. The way we putting our bodies on the line

72

for Lucille only to get criticized by the same people we fighting for. Like, damn! So yeah, we clap back sometimes."

Bitter stepped away from Eddie, embarrassed. "I'm sorry," she said. "I thought you were judging us."

"I mean, some Assata kids probably are, but it is what it is. The real question is, are you judging yourself for not having more capacity than you have?" Eddie tapped on her own chest. "That's what you gotta figure out, in there. Who you're really mad at. Us? Or yourself? And whatever system's got you thinking you have to do or be everything instead of just finding your pocket and fighting from it. Like, imagine if everyone did that—just found their pockets and fought for the revolution however best they could, within their capacity."

"Like Aloe and his healing," Bitter said thoughtfully.

"Yeah, exactly! He's wonderful at sound, sure, but man . . ." Eddie shook her head. "You should see him when he doing healing work, B. That's a whole different person. Like he's calm now, but when he's working, it's surreal. I ain't never seen nothing like it. Aloe be moving like nothing can touch him, like he anointed or some shit. He ain't scared of nothing, no one's getting left behind. You look at him and you know that healers are soldiers too."

Bitter narrowed her eyes. "You sounding real fond of him, oui?"

Eddie laughed and flopped down on Bitter's bed. She looked so comfortable there that it made Bitter's chest twinge a little. "Nah," Eddie was saying. "You know I don't do boys. He's all yours."

Bitter gave her a crooked smile and leaned her hip against the desk. "Thanks," she said sarcastically. "I appreciate it."

Eddie sketched out a small bow, bending just her head. "You're welcome. I think he's good for you, anyway."

"Yeah?"

"You're not as . . . spiky as you used to be."

Bitter blushed as she blurted out a confession. "He helps me feel safe. Like Blessing."

Eddie beamed. "See, that's important. I'm dating someone now who makes me feel like that too."

"Oh, really? What's she like?"

"Her name's Malachite. She's just . . . sweet and kind, you know? Feels like you wanna take care of her."

"What's her skill?" Bitter caught herself. "Sorry. I talking like she a Eucalyptus kid."

"Nah, it's cool. She grows food, works with the land, that kinda shit. Bakes fresh bread."

"That sounds extremely wholesome."

"It really is. Reminds me that we still gotta live, even while we fighting, you know?"

Bitter smiled. "I'm glad you have that."

Eddie smiled back, her walls down. "Me too. And I'm glad Aloe made us talk. It was fun hating you, don't get me wrong, but I think I'd like us better as friends."

"Okay, deal." Bitter reached out a fist, and Eddie dapped her. "Friends."

"Bet." Eddie looked around the room. "Now can we do the studio visit part? I gotta admit, I been curious about your art from jump—idk if Aloe woulda been able to get me here if he didn't bribe me with a tour of your work."

Bitter blushed again. She hadn't known Eddie had been interested in her work at all, but then again, she'd worked very hard to keep Eddie out of her life back then. "Sure," she said. "Let's start over here. But doh judge—these are really old. Like from before I came to Eucalyptus old."

"Ooh, we doing a deep dive! I'm here for it." Eddie hopped off the bed, and Bitter pulled out one of her early portfolios, fragments from her old life that made up the foundation of who she'd become.

She showed Eddie the first painting, made of feathers and wax and ash. It was small enough to slip into a pocket, from back when Bitter needed to both hide her work and make sure she could run with it at any moment. Eddie held the piece in both hands, cradling it gently like it could splinter apart if her breath touched it. One of her braids had slipped free from its bun and hung softly against the curve of her neck.

"Wow," she whispered, lifting her eyes to meet Bitter's. "This is amazing, B." Just like that, a warm bud unfurled between them, and as Bitter began to show her the rest of the work, she could feel something like friendship start to blossom again. Aloe was going to be so proud, she thought, but in that moment, Bitter was proud of herself for opening up and being honest, for doing the work to heal instead of believing things always had to stay broken.

CHAPTER 6

- - - - - - - - - - -

"I never thought I'd live to see you settle down," Blessing said, wiping a fake tear from the corner of her eye. "It's so beautiful."

Bitter shoved her. "Steups, man. It's not that serious."

"Y'all are attached at the hip—fuck you mean, it's not that serious? You cut off all your hoes, got these dudes going through withdrawal—shit, that sounds serious to me."

"Big facts," Alex chimed in. It was after classes, and the girls were out in the garden on a large picnic blanket, passing a joint around. Blessing was in a full floral set—from her hijab to her bright sweatsuit and holographic sneakers. The air outside was crisp and cool. Alex had her head on Blessing's thighs and was playing with the edge of her headscarf. "I'm just impressed you made up with Eddie. She and I go way back."

Bitter took a drag and blew the smoke up into the sky, trying to keep her face expressionless. This was the closest Alex had ever gotten to admitting that she'd been part of Assata. It was like reconnecting with Eddie had brought Bitter into Alex's inner circle, made her trust Bitter more, which made sense, knowing Assata and how insular they were. "Eddie's a sweetheart," she said. "We going for a walk later—she said she wants me to try sweet potato pie."

Blessing took the joint from her. "You've never had it before? The chef's definitely made it here."

Bitter made a face. "Yeah, but . . . what sweet potato doing in a pie?"

Alex snorted in laughter. "Bless your heart," she said. "I bet she's gonna take you over by Mrs. Nelson. That's the best pie in Lucille."

"I doh know that restaurant," Bitter said, and this time Blessing laughed.

"It's not a restaurant," she explained. "She sells home-made pies out of her kitchen. Her lemon meringue is out of this world. I would kidnap a small child for it."

"Yeah, her husband's the watermelon man." Alex stretched in the sun like a cat. "When it's cold, we get pies. When it's hot, we get watermelons."

"We can still get pies when it's hot," Blessing corrected.

"Yeah, but who wants pie when you could have *watermelon*?"

Bitter listened to them bickering, a small smile on her

face. She did know the watermelon man, Mr. Nelson. He'd shown her his harvest of different mini watermelons last summer, from the bright yellow Lemon Drop to the snow-white Silver Yamato. Bitter had bought one of the Lemon Drops, and it had tasted like sugar and sunlight.

"Hey," Blessing cut in, leaning over to hand Bitter the joint. "Alex and I are gonna join Eddie at the protest today."

She didn't say anything else, but Bitter could hear the invitation simmering under the surface of her words. Blessing had mentioned that maybe being in a pod of people she knew would make protests easier for Bitter, like some kind of exposure therapy, but Bitter was firmly against the idea. Lucille's protests could become a regular part of everyone else's life, but that didn't mean she had to make it part of her own world, not when she'd done so much work to keep it out. It was too dangerous, and she didn't want a life where danger was a normal thing you just walked willingly into.

"You already know I staying right here," she said, and Blessing shrugged.

"You know, I think it's scarier when you're inside all the time," Alex chimed in. "Like, your imagination makes it out to be all these things, but if you checked it out in person, it might not be that bad."

"Or it might be worse!" Bitter shot her a dark look. "Doh be acting like it doh get bad out there."

"Bitter's right," Blessing said. "People have different reactions to shit. Like, you cool with getting arrested and all, no sweat, but someone else would have a complete panic attack."

Bitter raised her hand. "Me. I would have a complete panic attack. Getting arrested sounds terrifying."

Alex laughed with far too much ease for the subject of conversation. Bitter wondered how many times the cops had thrown her into the back of their black wagons. "Fair enough," she said. "But Lucille keeps fighting even if you try not to look at it. Eucalyptus is right in the middle of everything, anyway."

Bitter winced. "Don't remind me."

Alex checked the time and swore loudly. "Shit, I'm late for my studio visit." She scrambled up and kissed Blessing before heading off through the garden, past the rows of hibiscus bushes. Bitter passed the joint over to Blessing.

"I wish I was the type of person who could go," she said.

Blessing stretched out on the blanket and blew smoke rings into the sky. "You good either way, babe."

Bitter sighed and looked out over the garden lawn, her face brightening as she saw Eddie heading toward them. "Eddie's here!" she said, climbing to her feet. The last thing she wanted was more protest talk between Blessing and Eddie. "I'll go meet her and we'll link later?"

Blessing waved a nonchalant hand. "Sounds good," she said, her voice drifting off as she gazed into the sky. Bitter chuckled and grabbed her things, then jogged across the grass to get to Eddie.

"Hey, you ready for our walk?" she asked as she and Eddie hugged.

"Yeah, but I was gonna say hi to Blessing first."

"She's in another world right now—doh even worry about it."

Eddie laughed. "Aight. You ready to have your mind blown?"

The girls linked arms as they left Eucalyptus, and Bitter tried not to think about how fragile the peace around them was, how violently the protest later would inevitably break it. Sometimes she wasn't sure which of the two worlds she lived in was going to drive her mad first.

"This better be the most magical pie I ever tasted," she shot back. "Or else I go question your taste for the rest of time."

Eddie puffed herself up. "Oh, I'm sure," she said. "Mrs. Nelson is a Lucille legend for a reason."

"Yeah, Alex was telling me about her. I met her husband last summer. Has he always been the watermelon man?"

"Yup. He used to run a farm stand year-round, but then Theron started pushing out all the mom-and-pops with that organic food chain, and Mr. Nelson just . . . ran out of business." A faint cloud passed over Eddie's face. "I heard stories that someone was fucking with his crops too, but the Nelsons don't like to talk about things like that." She shook off the cloud and smiled at Bitter. "You'll see. Mrs. Nelson is the sweetest old lady in the world."

They turned down the street the Nelsons lived on, and Eddie pointed out their house—a quaint sky-blue cottage with a white picket fence and flowers tumbling everywhere.

"Their old farm's a few miles outside Lucille," Eddie said as they walked up the path to the front door and rang the bell. "It's mostly lying fallow now." Bitter raised an eyebrow and Eddie blushed. "Malachite taught me that. She helps them out once in a while, whenever they need it."

"When do I get to meet her?" Bitter asked.

"Soon as she's back from her herbalism course, we're all gonna go on what—a triple date? It's gon' be lit."

The front door opened, and an old man with incredibly kind eyes and deep butterscotch skin was looking down at them. His gaze rested on Eddie, and his face wrinkled with a grin. "Hey there, trouble," he said. "You bringing more trouble to my house?"

"Well, of course, Mr. Nelson. If I don't bring you trouble, who's gon' come trouble you? Can't leave you out here all bored and untroubled, now."

Mr. Nelson's laugh was sharp and rich. "Welcome," he said

to Bitter. "Y'all come on in." He stepped away from the door, and Bitter followed Eddie into the warmth of the house. The floor was hardwood, polished and dark with age, and solid ceiling beams stretched from wall to wall. The air smelled like cinnamon and spices, a thick welcome that made Bitter's mouth water. Mr. Nelson walked with a slight limp, favoring his left leg as he led them to an enormous kitchen with butcher-block countertops and copper pans hanging over the stove. "Y'all here for some pie, right?"

Eddie swung herself onto a kitchen stool, and Bitter sat next to her. "Yeah—she's never had sweet potato pie, Mr. Nelson."

He gasped and clutched at his chest, turning amused eyes to Bitter. "Thank God my wife isn't here to hear that blasphemy, child! How your people never made you pie?"

Bitter ducked her head, the mention of her people bringing back cold flashes of lost years. "I was adopted," she said, not even sure whether that counted as a lie or not. It was certainly better than saying she was a foster orphan no one had wanted before Eucalyptus.

Eddie placed a hand on her knee, and Mr. Nelson gave them a shrewd look but didn't push. "Matter of fact," he said, pulling out a pie and beginning to cut slices of it, "it's a good thing your first time is going to be my Ethel's recipe. It don't get no better than this."

"Where is Miss Ethel?" Eddie asked, her eyes fixed on the pie he was lifting onto plates.

"Out by the Jacksons. Their little girl's been doing poorly of late." He glanced over at Eddie. "I think you know her brother—he's an Assata kid, like you."

Eddie's face lit up. "Oh yeah, Chijioke! He did say his sister's been sick." Just as quickly, her face dropped and her jaw tensed up. "Their apartment complex is one of those in the lawsuit against Theron's real estate company."

Mr. Nelson put the girls' plates in front of them with a clang. "Now, Eddie," he said, and his voice was light but his eyes had hardened. "You know we don't say that demon's name in this house."

Eddie lowered her gaze and picked up her fork. "Yes, sir. I'm sorry."

Bitter glanced back and forth between them, a little confused by the undercurrents of unsaid things. It was Theron, though—filling in the gaps wasn't difficult. She could vaguely remember Blessing and Alex talking about the conditions of Theron's apartment complexes, but if this was what it sounded like, things there were bad enough to make a little girl very sick. A sour coating washed over Bitter's tongue. This was the Lucille she didn't want to look at, a dark hole that would swallow her up entirely if she let it. How on earth did Eddie fight against that suction, that pulling despair?

Mr. Nelson sat across the kitchen counter from them and smiled at Eddie, his eyes soft again. "Ethel and I, we are so proud of you kids, you know? It breaks our hearts to know that you fighting the same damn fight we fought back in the day, but shit, that's how it goes. A war that spans generations, and y'all are the fiercest fighters yet." He pointed a finger at her, and Bitter could almost feel the force of his belief and care radiating in the air toward Eddie. "Don't ever doubt what you're doing. It's important. It's worth it. We need every single body that's out there—it all counts." He leaned back and folded his arms. "Your leaders are doing a fine job, the young ones. The Elders too, but y'all youngsters are something special."

Eddie sat with her fork in her hand, her pie untouched and her eyes damp. "Well, technically we don't have leaders," she said, her voice straining to be light under the weight of emotion.

Bitter did a double take. "Yeah, you do. Isn't that what Ube is?"

Eddie twirled her fork and smiled. "Nah. Assata is led by Assata. Ube is just . . . he got a lot of force in his spirit, and he got a way with words."

"He got that divine anointing, that's what he got," said Mr. Nelson. "We can all see it."

"Yeah." Eddie shrugged. "Something like that. Ube is

special, and he reminds us where our hearts should be when we forget or get carried away."

Bitter frowned. "But you don't actually have to do what he says?"

"Nah." Eddie leaned in and inhaled the scent of the pie. "See, if Assata doesn't have a head, then you can't chop the head off. Leaders are dangerous. One person is weak; the people are strong."

Mr. Nelson laughed. "Ain't that a word. You better dig into that pie before you eat it all up with your eyes, Eddie— I see you."

Eddie grinned at him. "I'm just waiting for Bitter to appreciate all the elements of this pie. Take a deep breath, B."

Bitter obeyed, leaning in and closing her eyes. It smelled sweet with an edge of spice, warm, and she could almost taste the crumble of the crust.

"There you go," Eddie said. "Now we dig in."

The girls took their first forkfuls of pie, with both Eddie and Mr. Nelson watching Bitter to see her reaction. She had a moment of feeling self-conscious, but then the flavors ignited on her tongue and Bitter made a low, appreciative sound in her throat. "Oh, that's good!" she said.

"See?" Eddie was smiling victoriously. "And now your life has changed."

After Eddie dropped her off back at the school and left for the protest, Bitter couldn't stop thinking about the conversation at the Nelsons' house. Every single body counted, Mr. Nelson had said. One person was weak, Eddie had said, and it made Bitter think about her life before Eucalyptus. She knew she had been strong—you couldn't survive lost years like that without being strong—but it wasn't the same strength as what she had now with her friends. She had been more fragile then, maybe, just trying to survive. Less protected, less safe. *The people are strong.* Bitter couldn't imagine what it was like to be out there as a protest drew in breath, to look around and see the faces of people who had chosen to fight beside you, to know that you all were comrades together, even if you didn't live to see the next morning. It was a bravery her friends knew; they were gathering right now: Blessing and Alex, Aloe and Eddie. They'd look around and see each other. Bitter wanted to be with them, but she very much wished that didn't have to mean being in the middle of Lucille as it went up in a righteous spark.

Still, she imagined how Eddie's face would light up to see her, how proud Aloe would be. Blessing would be so excited, and Alex would approve. Wasn't that part of growth, to push yourself outside your comfort zone? To show up for the people you cared about? If she went early, before the protest start time, maybe she could see her friends and then be back in Eucalyptus before things got too heated. Eddie had shown her the route they were taking on her phone, and the intersection they were gathering at was right around the corner from the school. Bitter thought she could make it. It would be a brief showing, just enough so the people she cared about knew that she cared enough to *really* try. They'd understand when she slipped away, back to where it was safe.

With her mind made up, she moved quickly so it didn't change back. Bitter pulled on some plain sweats, laced up her running shoes, and threw some energy bars into her backpack for her friends, grabbing a full water bottle as she left her room. Her door closed behind her with a gentle click, and she kept her feet soft as she went down the stairs, unlatched the main door, and stepped out into the Eucalyptus grounds. Evening was wrapping the air in a faint chill, and the sun was swollen and orange. Bitter pushed her hands into her pockets, trying to calm the thudding of her heart as she made her way along the gravel paths. It was going to be fine. She could do this, go out there, be out there, for Blessing, for Aloe, for Eddie. Maybe she should have told Aloe she was going, asked him to come with her, but he was on his whole protest medic thing—he'd be busy, and Bitter didn't want to feel like he was babysitting her. She could do this alone.

By the time she got to the side gate, her pulse was chaos rattling in her ears and her chest was getting tight, making it hard to take a deep breath. Bitter had to stop and brace herself against a wall, biting down on her lip as she forced herself to breathe, to not give up even though ghosts of sirens and screams were playing in her head: the sound of people running; clips from videos she'd seen one time too many; the casual ease with which a cop aimed pepper spray at a child's face; the body covered in the middle of the street for hours, cordoned off by caution tape, his mother screaming on the border. Bitter's vision went blurry as panic made a small tornado in her chest, knifing her body over and stealing blood from her numb fingertips. The feeling arrived too fast to stop, as it always did, drowning her and squeezing her heart so tight, she was entirely certain that if she took a step out of the gate, out of the safety of Eucalyptus, her heart would stop and she would die. She had to turn around, she had to go back to her room and lock the door, press a heavy chair against it to block out the forces on the outside, the hungry city of Lucille, eager to eat all its citizens. Bitter was running before she knew it, not out there to her friends but back into the building, back into the belly of the old brick, up the stairs and into her room, slamming the door behind her as she tore off the backpack and threw it down with a cry of helpless rage. The walls still felt too far away, too useless, and Bitter was crying now, big gulping sobs as she dropped to her knees, her palms hitting the floor, the impact dull and dead. She curled into a tight ball and screamed into her legs, sobbing until her chest loosened and her heart decided not to crush itself.

Time unspun into textures, the wood against her cheek, the cotton of her sweats against her damp skin. Colorful circles brightened and dimmed behind her eyelids, salt dried on her face, and the muscles of her arms stayed locked around herself. Everything outside her room, outside the puddle she was in on the floor, it all melted away. Bitter used to do this inside the lost years, in those houses she didn't remember anymore, curling and floating away until the pain wasn't real anymore, until nothing was real and she was lost inside a kind of trance that bled smoothly into a halfway sleep.

Hours could vanish like this, warped away in a place her mind had made safe, so by the time Bitter uncurled herself and sat up, she wasn't surprised to see that the day had already gone into deep dusk, a touch away from dark. She dragged her hands over her face, then pushed herself off the floor, scrambling unsteadily to her feet. Nothing felt quite real. She grabbed her backpack from where it was slumped against her closet door and emptied it onto her bed, her phone falling out in a shower of energy bars. Bitter woke her screen up and winced at the number of notifications she'd missed. Aloe had called several times, texted her to call him, then left a bunch of voice notes. Bitter hit play on the first one.

"*B, I've been trying to call you—*" Aloe's voice was drowned out in a wave of chaotic sound, people yelling, sirens, and then an explosion. "*Shit! Stay inside, okay, B? Tonight's not good—things are really bad. I need you to stay inside— Pull back, pull back! More milk, pass me more milk, it's all in his eyes, shit— B, I gotta go. Stay inside, okay? I'll be back as soon as I can.*"

The background sounds were everything Bitter was afraid of. She wondered what had gone wrong, what had escalated, but this was Lucille—everything always escalated, even if it started out peacefully. You couldn't predict what the police would do, when they'd hold defense or when they'd swarm like soldiers of death. It kept everyone on edge, jumpy, the way they liked it. There was no peace.

She listened to the second voice note, telling her that Blessing and Alex were headed back to the school, then to the fragmented ones that came after that, alarm building in her with a hot urgency. There had to be a mistake—she couldn't have heard that right, what Aloe had said about Eddie. She was playing his voice again when the phone rang with a call from him. Bitter answered immediately.

"Where are you?" she asked. "Where's Eddie?"

"Where the hell are you?" he replied, his voice taut with relief. "I've been trying to get hold of you from since."

"In my room. I didn't go out. But, Aloe—"

"I'm coming upstairs now. See you soon." He hung up, and Bitter stared at her phone, some of the tension easing now that she knew he was back inside Eucalyptus. Maybe he was wrong about what he'd seen, maybe he'd made a mistake and he was going to walk in and tell her it was all okay, it was all a misunderstanding.

Aloe knocked on the door once before pushing it open, and Bitter threw herself into his arms. "You're okay," she whispered. "You're here."

He hugged her tightly but didn't say anything. Bitter looked over his shoulder, as if Eddie was going to be right behind him, smirk on her face, her braid spikes clattering between her shoulder blades. "Where's Eddie?" she asked. He had to tell her there'd been a mistake.

Aloe held her even more tightly, as if that could stop her from spinning out. "Eddie's going to be okay," he said, but there was no confidence in his voice.

Bitter pulled away from him. "No. You said—you said they shot her!"

"With a rubber bullet."

"How does that matter? They *shot* her!"

"She's alive." Aloe's voice was somber, and it brought Bitter down to earth like she'd been thrown from a building. "I mean that Eddie's alive. It could have been worse."

Bitter's eyes went hot with tears. "What did the hospital say?"

There were shadows under and inside his eyes. Aloe stepped away from Bitter and slumped down in the gray armchair. "They shot her in the face, B."

Bitter felt her legs give out, dropping her gently onto her bed. "What?"

"It was on purpose. The doctors, they said she might lose her eye."

"They shot her in her *face*?"

He passed a hand over his mouth. "Yes. I just—" Aloe shook his head, unable to form more words.

There was a sick weight in Bitter's stomach, and she didn't know what to do with it. "Is she having surgery?"

"I don't know. That was the last update I got. You know how Assata is. They're not talking to outsiders right now."

"That's bullshit! You been working as a protest medic *for* them."

"It is what it is. They have protocols, and she's one of their own. Ube said he'll text me as soon as they know more."

Bitter scoffed. "And yuh believe him?"

The look Aloe shot at her was cutting. "Of course I believe him, Bitter."

She bit her lip, flushing at the censure in his tone. "Sorry. I'm just—"

"It's fine. It's a hard time for everyone, and she's your friend too."

Bitter sank down to the floor, leaning against her bed, the base of her skull digging into the frame. "She's my friend," she repeated. "Could you imagine it?"

Aloe gave a short laugh. "I'm as amazed as you are. I thought you two were going to kill each other at first."

Bitter tried to smile, but her mouth couldn't quite make it. "The girl like a cyst, you know. She does grow on you."

Aloe looked over, then slid off the armchair and sat next to her, leaning his thigh and shoulder against hers. "How are you feeling?"

Bitter didn't look at him. "I'm fine," she bit out. "I was in here, safe and sound, while Eddie was getting shot in the face."

"Bitter . . ."

"No, it's true. I wanted to come out, just this once, and I couldn't even manage that."

Aloe took her hand in his. "You don't have to come out. We've told you that."

"Well, I still feeling like ah little bitch for staying in."

He made a sharp annoyed sound. "Don't talk like that. Remember what Eddie said—we all have a role to play."

"A role?!" Bitter pushed up from the floor and paced the room. "I doh have no fucking role, Aloe. All I doing is drawing pictures while you out there helping people and Eddie out there fighting for us. I eh doing nothing!"

"That's not true—" Aloe broke off as his phone vibrated. He looked at the screen, and Bitter saw his jaw tense up.

"What is it?"

Aloe turned the screen toward her, and Bitter flinched when she saw the photo of Eddie, her face swollen and almost unrecognizable beneath gauze and bandages. "Ube said she's lost the eye," Aloe said, and a thick oily feeling started in Bitter's stomach, hot and ugly and hateful.

"No . . . ," she whispered. Aloe was already standing up as he texted back. "Not Eddie, she can't have—"

"I have to go. They're taking her home, and Ube's requested some supplies I was meant to bring by."

"Okay, I'll come with you." Bitter started looking around for her jacket, but Aloe's hand on her arm stopped her.

"It's still Assata only," he said, his voice gentle.

Bitter pulled her arm away, stung. "You're not Assata."

"I know. I'm just doing a drop-off. Besides, the protests haven't stopped."

Bitter blinked in shock. "What?"

"Yeah, they cleared out the center, but Assata's Elders got people pushing in from the sides. You're safer indoors, Bitter. I'll be faster on my own. I'll make it to Ube and back before you know it."

The panic was fluttering inside her now, its wings coated with thick, angry oil. What if he didn't make it back to Eucalyptus? "Why haven't they stopped?" she asked, her voice shaky. "They usually stop."

Aloe pocketed his phone, his expression grim. "I don't think anyone's stopping this time," he said.

"But the protests can't go on forever."

There was something in Aloe's eyes that Bitter had seen before, in Eddie and in Ube and sometimes when Alex actually got to talking. It was determined and bleak and hopeful all at once.

"We have nothing but time," Aloe said before pulling her into a hug and kissing her forehead, his lips smooth against her skin. "Stay here. I need you to be safe. Call Blessing."

"I think she's still out there with Alex—she would've come by my room if she was back."

Aloe frowned. "I talked to her right before I called you. She's safe—she's not at the protest. Don't worry, they'll be back soon. Just stay inside Eucalyptus, okay?"

Bitter nodded, and then he was gone and she was

standing there, Eddie's face scorched into her mind, boiling oil puddling in her belly. It rose up slowly inside her as she remembered Eddie laughing, Eddie looking at her paintings, Eddie taking her hand and reminding her that everyone had a role to play. Bitter could feel the old urge itching under her fingernails, but this time it was furious, not lonely. This time it wanted to fight, it wanted to punish the monsters for breaking the peace of her bubble, for hurting her friend, for everything they were doing, thinking they were unstoppable, thinking no one was big enough or powerful enough or rich enough to make them stop. Blessing had been right. Not everything was about money.

Some things were about blood.

CHAPTER 7

- - - - - - - - - - - - -

An hour later, Bitter's arm was aching from the force of what she was drawing, but she couldn't stop. The jagged wooden panel leaning against her wall had a figure sketched out on it in chalk and ash, muddled whites and grays. She and Blessing had found the huge piece of wood outside a few weeks ago, and it had taken the two of them to carry it back to Eucalyptus. They'd brushed all the dirt and debris off before taking it upstairs. Bitter had thought it would be useful if she ever wanted to make a painting that size, but she hadn't been ready back then. Things were different now, though, and all that furious oil simmering inside her had to go somewhere. It felt like if she didn't push it out through her hands, it was going to smother her heart, drown her in the despair of living somewhere like Lucille, where people were being hurt so often, in so many directions that you couldn't keep track of it all, you couldn't grieve it all, you were always catching up and falling behind, and how was this supposed to be a life? There was a sheet spread out on the floor below the wood, and Bitter wasn't even sure she had enough materials for what she wanted to make, but she was determined to use every drop of anything she could find. For Eddie, for want of a world without monsters.

Fumio Itabashi's "Watarase" was playing on an endless loop, maddened streaks of piano trilling through the air, washing away everything outside the walls so that it was only Bitter and the hot oil flooding her heart and the wood and her arm striking across it. To her surprise, the rage didn't feel heated as it worked its way out of her. If felt cold, certain as ice, dark as deep water. Her desire was clear—she wanted the monsters gone. Assata had been fighting for this for as long as she could remember, their Elders before them, for the same thing, and how long was everyone supposed to wait? James Baldwin had asked this question years and years before; so had Lena Horne; so had thousands of tired people who just wanted to live. How much time was it going to take? Bitter drew more bold lines with the chalk, thick and white across the wood, shadowing a face in gray, filling in the long neck, the wide, wide mouth, a stain of turmeric and charcoal for the eyes. The figure was folded in, flattening itself out over the grain of the wood. The panel was too small for what it was; it needed more space than it had. It was crammed, hemmed in, cramped and trapped and angry about it. Bitter got lost in its form, cloudy and textured.

She stepped back and looked at it, the music racing like a river through her veins, white foam and speckled water. The figure wasn't even close to enough. Bitter maneuvered the wood panel down to the floor, on top of the sheet, so it spilled like a pool at her feet. That felt better, like it was under her hands now. She reached for a brush and a small tub of white casein paint, falling back into the figure, as the piano swept lightly over deep bass notes, over and over again, and the hours went by. Bitter added wax and eggshells, intermittent fragments of smooth gloss within the figure's coat. She burned sheets of paper to make more ash, letting the flakes drop onto the wet paint, filling up every inch of the wood, layering the figure's shape on top of itself, and at some point Bitter realized she was sobbing, her tears splashing on the painting, but she didn't stop and the piano didn't stop because the people out there hadn't stopped so nothing, really, nothing could stop.

When, finally, the figure was almost complete, Bitter fell back against the edge of her bed. Her muscles were sore and exhausted; she had no idea how long she'd been painting. The figure was roiling inside the wood, like an imprisoned cloud with a dark, wide mouth. Bitter stared at it numbly, her face tracked with dried salt from all the crying she'd done. She should have been afraid of what she was about to do, but there was nothing that could scare her inside her bubble. They had shot Eddie, taken her eye. They had killed more people than anyone even knew about. No matter what Bitter could imagine, the monsters had done worse. It didn't make her happy to paint something that could be more terrible than them—that wasn't something to be proud of—but she wouldn't know until the painting was complete, and there was only one thing left to do.

Bitter reached out and grabbed a precision knife from her supplies. In movies, people were always cutting their palms, but that seemed like a terrible idea, because then she wouldn't be able to use that hand until it healed, and also, that would take forever to close up. Bitter knelt in front of the painting, the knife hovering over her left forearm. She wanted to do it quickly, but that wasn't how these kinds of things worked. She'd never needed this much blood before— usually a pinprick would do it—but this figure was larger than anything she'd ever made, hungrier than anything she'd ever made, and Bitter wanted to make sure it was also more powerful than her little silent creatures that faded away so fast. She took a deep breath, and as the piano dug into a crescendo, she sliced the skin of her forearm open with a quick stroke. It gaped palely at her for a moment before rushing red with blood, pain yelling up her nerves. Bitter gasped and tears stung her eyes as she watched the blood spill over her skin. She held her arm over the painting and gritted her teeth from the pain as the blood dripped into the ash and chalk and wax, spreading in bright blurred circles. Her heart was racing, pounding like it knew she'd opened her flesh up, like it was trying to make up for the blood she was using. Bitter dropped the knife and cupped her right hand under the cut, letting the blood collect in her palm, crying quietly. It hurt so fucking much, but it didn't hurt as much as what they'd done to Eddie or as much as what it felt like to be alive at a time like this.

She closed her eyes and for once let herself feel *everything*. Not just what was happening in Lucille to people who looked like her, not just what they'd done to all the kids like Eddie, but also the darkness of the years she'd forgotten, the boy hunting her while she hid in the attic, his hands in her hair, the foster parents who called her and her mother cursed, the shame of knowing her father was a monster, which meant monster blood ran in her, but that was fine because if it took monster blood to get rid of the monsters, then Bitter was ready to do her part, her terrible and necessary part, no more hiding in Eucalyptus, no more staying apart and uninvolved. Her mother was dead and her father was a monster and Bitter didn't know what she was, but she knew what she could *do*, she knew it was powerful and she was tired of being scared. Maybe it was time to become the scary one, the one they ran from, the one who could hurt those who thought they were untouchable. Nothing was untouchable. Bitter knew this because of everything that had already been taken from her. The foster parents had said she would end up nowhere, and she didn't even mind, because if you were nowhere, then you could make up wherever you wanted to be, you could make it real. You could, for example, paint it into existence.

And right now, Bitter wanted to be safe and protected, she wanted to matter more than the money that people like Theron used as a weapon, she wanted all of them to matter more than the money. The blood was a red mirror in her hand. Bitter let all the hurt and rage and want flood up her throat and out past her teeth and lips. She screamed as loudly as she could and slapped her hand full of blood down on the painting, right over the figure's wide, wide mouth. It was so wet under her palm.

"Come out," she ordered. "Come out and *play.*" There was a wealth of anger in that last word, but she didn't regret it because these monsters, you see, it was all a game to them. Eddie's eye was a game, the protests and the deaths and the suffering weren't real because the people weren't real to them, to Dian Theron and men like him, whose ancestors

had owned people and boasted about it with statues all over Lucille. Assata and the Elders had ruined the statues righteously, splashing them with red paint, pulling one or two down, the heavy stone crashing against the street, but what happened to the alive monsters like Theron? Those who kept playing with people like lives didn't matter. Bitter wanted them to feel what it was like to be on the other end of it, and she put all that sour rage into her hand and her voice and her order.

It took only a few seconds for the figure to stir, its wide mouth drinking in her blood, smearing it down its chin and neck. Bitter snatched her hand away and scrambled backward, watching the painting with fascinated horror. She'd never seen one this big come to life, and she hadn't even been sure that it would, despite all the energy she'd poured into it. A groaning sound came out from the wood, and the edges of the panel began to buckle and warp. The muddy white of the figure lifted up from the surface, ballooning into the air, then it flattened back down with a wet slap before ballooning up again. It looked like it was breathing, and Bitter realized it was *trying* to come forth, pushing as hard as it could. Itabashi was still playing on repeat over her speakers, the volume blasting as loud as it could go, surreal birds chirping as the painting tried to break through. Goose bumps raced up Bitter's legs.

"Come out!" she yelled, her arm a scream of pain. She wanted it to *live*. She wanted it to be everything she'd hoped and wept for, a weapon for the people, and it would mean that she had done something right, she'd helped instead of watching everyone fight on the front lines. "Come out and play!" The words felt like knives in her mouth, cutting her tongue with despair and malice. The painting groaned back, a deep and restructuring sound. Its head broke free of the wood, splinters flying into the air, and Bitter flinched. The figure was much larger than she'd expected—its scaled head alone was about half the size of her body, with seven narrow and opaque eyes, all a feline yellow with black slits. Its neck snaked out from the painting, a streak of wax gleaming down its red throat, jagged white eggshells marking its spine, going on forever before the torso emerged with a slick hiss.

The creature looked like it was made out of compressed smoke that was having a hard time staying together; it kept giving off thick gouts of gray and white that would then pull back to the body. It was already eclipsing Bitter's room, its head bending against her ceiling as the rest of its body broke out of the wood, long limbs and hooked claws. An acrid smell filled the air, and Bitter noticed that the wooden panel was charring as the creature worked its way through. She stared in shock as the wood burned, as this thing unfolded in front of her, terrifying and absolutely too big for this world. Her desk was pushed aside, then her bed and armchair, all the furniture scraping across the floor as the figure swelled into the room. Bitter pressed her back against the wall, speechless. It was going to crush her, she realized, it was going to crush her, explode out of her room, and collapse the building. Miss Virtue was going to be fucking pissed.

"Stop!" she yelled above the crackling smoke and agonized wood. "Yuh growing too much—stop!"

To her surprise, the figure paused. Its face snaked around on that unnaturally long neck before the seven eyes found her, and the wide mouth stretched even wider, dark with her own blood.

"Child," it said, and its voice was like glass stabbing through her head. Bitter cried out and covered her ears. The figure tilted its head, the mouth still obscenely open.

"That hurt," Bitter choked out. "A lot."

The figure made a low-pitched rolling sound, and Bitter watched as its body contracted down into a size that could fit her room. It was still unimaginably large—she had to crane her neck back to be able to look up at it. It dragged the rest of its body out of the painting, leaving a charred hole in the middle of the wood panel. Bitter could see that the sheet underneath was singed, and she said a quick and futile prayer to no one in particular that the floor wasn't damaged, because she had no idea how she'd explain that to Miss

Virtue. The creature's several eyes looked at Bitter without blinking, out of that scaled and shifting face, the chasm of its mouth perpetually stretched as wisps of smoke drifted off it and dispersed into the air.

"Child," it said again, but this time its voice didn't hurt. It was low, too low to be from this world, guttural and thick, like something that had been dead for a very long time. Still, Bitter wasn't afraid. She'd been alone for too long to be afraid now, and all the things she made were hers, no matter how scary they looked. They were born from her head and her hands and her monster child blood.

"My name is Bitter," she said, taking a small step toward it, curious now. None of her paintings had ever spoken to her before, but this one was never meant to be like the rest. "I made you."

The creature slithered along her walls, repositioning itself away from the charred wood. "I know," it said. "I am the first."

"No, I does make paintings come alive all the time," Bitter corrected.

The creature looked at her with its flat eyes. "I am the first," it repeated, lowering its head to be level with hers. A cold feeling crossed the back of Bitter's neck. Was it disagreeing with her? Pushing back? They weren't supposed to do that.

"You the first like you," she conceded. Maybe it just didn't think the way she did. She'd never made one like it before, after all.

It rumbled low in its throat, then slid around her, knocking books off her shelf. A glass box fell to the ground and shattered.

"Watch yuhself!" Bitter scolded. The creature stopped; then its form rippled down its smoky length and it became a fraction more translucent, and suddenly nothing in the room was touching it. Bitter could see the dim outline of her desk through its body. She reached out and touched one of its limbs, gasping softly when her fingers sank through it, as if it was smoke. "Oh, wow. You could make yuhself like so? Less . . . solid?" It didn't reply, swerving its neck instead to look out of her window. Bitter glanced along with it. The sky outside was totally dark now, only flickering streetlights visible through her blinds. "That's Lucille," she said. "It's where I live."

It suddenly occurred to her that if this one could talk back, then maybe it could answer some of the questions she'd been holding for years. "Where yuh come from?" she asked. "Why the blood does call you?" The creature ignored her completely, and Bitter felt that cold warning again. Something *was* different about this one. "Why did you come?" she ventured.

This time it swiveled its neck to look at her with that marbled gaze. "Show me your arm," it said. Bitter hesitated, then stretched her left arm out to the creature. The cut she'd made was still seeping blood, and just reaching out pulled on the skin, making it hurt worse. She winced and fought back tears. The creature extended one of its smoky limbs, retracting its claws until only one was out, curved and sharp.

"Doh hurt me," Bitter whispered, suddenly afraid that it was going to rip her arm open some more, take all her blood for itself. She was too scared to move—there was nowhere to run to.

The creature paused, its yellow eyes flickering at her. "I would never hurt you, child." It touched its claw to her forearm, and the tip of it sank into her skin like a dream. There was no pain at first, just an increasing warmth that seared down the length of the wound. Bitter gasped as the cut flared hot, then watched in shock as the flesh pulled itself back together, healing quickly. The creature removed its claw, and her arm wasn't on fire anymore, the cut wasn't there anymore.

Bitter looked up at it. "Thank you," she said, pulling her arm back and cradling it against her chest. "Yuh eh have to do that."

"You bled for me," the creature replied, swiveling its

scaled head around. The broken eggshells on its spine glinted in the light.

Fair enough, Bitter thought. That entitled her to some answers, at least. "Why yuh here? What yuh want?"

"You called," it said. "You wanted."

"I know," she replied, "but what about you?"

The creature opened its mouth and its voice glitched, the guttural rot falling out of it. A smooth and menacing deep voice replaced it, melodic with an icy charm. "Child, you *wanted* what I am." It glanced out of the window again, almost distracted.

Bitter took another step. "Okay," she said. "What *are* you?" She needed to know everything she could, because suddenly the power balance in the room had shifted into something she didn't quite recognize. Bitter was painfully aware that she was just a small human next to a very large and intimidating creature that could toss her out of that window like a rag doll if it wanted to. She was hoping that it wouldn't, that it meant what it said about not hurting her, that they would have the connection she'd had with all her other little creatures—something fond, something that recognized it wouldn't have existed if she hadn't made it, something that made her matter to it. The creature barely seemed to be paying attention to her, and Bitter didn't like how separate it made her feel, how scared and lonely. "What do I call you?" she asked, forcing a smile on her face. Maybe if she seemed relaxed, she wouldn't tip it off to how nervous she was actually getting. "Do you have a name?"

It looked down at her without expression, those inhuman eyes blank as chalk. "What I am," it said. "Call me what I am. Call me what you wanted."

"I wanted help," Bitter said, keeping the smile plastered on her face. "Are you here to help?"

It tilted its head again; then Bitter felt the force of its full attention home in on her, like a blast of cool, heavy air. She fought the urge to take a step backward. She had made this thing and she would face it.

"Help?" it repeated.

"Yes! With the monsters, Theron, the mayor." She threw up her hands and her smile left. "Everything!" Didn't it understand? Couldn't it feel how much she'd put into it, how much she was hurting, how much she needed things to change?

"Call me what you wanted," it repeated. "It was not help."

"Yes, it was!" Bitter almost stamped her foot, she was getting so frustrated.

The creature stared at her, then replicated the smile she'd worn just a moment ago, stretching its dark mouth wide, her blood dry and cracking at the corners. It was a chilling sight—it looked *wrong*, all seven eyes fixed on Bitter.

"Call me what you wanted, child," it said, amused and full of a lethal charm, its voice colder than dry ice. "Call me Vengeance."

CHAPTER 8

- - - - - - - - - - -

"That's not what I wanted!" Bitter protested, her fingers numb with adrenaline. She just wanted help. She wanted the monsters to be gone. She wanted Lucille to be safe, no matter how impossible that felt. "You meant to be, like, a protector. Can't I call you something else?"

Vengeance glanced out of the window again. "No," it said. "You wanted them to suffer."

"I—"

"We are paired by blood, little one. You cannot lie to me."

Bitter fell silent, then took a deep breath. "Do you know what they doing to us?"

Vengeance rippled. "Yes. Atrocities."

"Right. I just want it to stop."

The creature's body was still as it looked out into Lucille, smoke drifting off it. "You humans have always been like this. We have watched since the beginning."

"What you mean, *we*?"

"Us." Vengeance lowered its neck and rotated its head clockwise. "The angels."

Bitter thought she had heard wrong. "The *what*?"

It ignored her question. "It is a good thing you called us. We can reset things again."

She was starting to feel dangerously out of her depth. "What yuh talking about?" Her questions were piling up like a drowning wave in her head—Bitter couldn't keep track of them all. What did it mean by a reset? When had it done a reset before, and why did it keep talking as if there was more than one of it? What the hell did it mean by *angels*? The little things she had been drawing couldn't have been angels.

"Do not be afraid," Vengeance said. "The world changes when the angels return. You will see it, hear it. It will make its way into your language, it will bend the shape of your air." Vengeance stretched out, and Bitter backed up against the wall. "The hunters only hunt those who need hunting, those who cause harm and call down the hot light upon their heads."

"The world changes?" Bitter echoed, as if saying it again would help it make sense.

"It burns," Vengeance said, and its voice glitched back into the thick guttural sound, heavy and dead. "Worlds burn when the angels return."

Bitter scoffed for a second. "This world's already burning."

Vengeance turned to her and smiled again. "Yes," it crooned. "It is. It can burn even better."

Something about its assurance pulled at Bitter. It sounded like it had a vision. "What does better look like?" she asked.

The creature purred roughly, the sound wavering through its smoke. "Death," it said, and it made the word sound like every desire in the world was caught up in it, like it was everything anyone could ever want, like it had waited lifetimes to reach this point. It set off warning bells in Bitter's head.

"We have enough death," she said.

"Not enough," Vengeance replied. "I felt what you wanted. Theron. Your leaders. How many humans have died from them?"

"I don't—I don't know." The answer was *too many*. She was lying and she knew it, and if what Vengeance had hinted at was true, about being able to detect her lies, then it knew it as well.

"We agree with you. How much peace would their deaths bring?" Before Bitter could even think of a response, Vengeance reared up, and its smoke undulated in strong waves, directed out toward the window, toward Lucille. "We will hunt them. All monsters must die."

"Hold up nuh." Removing Theron's power was one thing;

115

killing him was another. "Can't you just take their money away or something? Redistribute it?"

Vengeance slowly turned its scaly head to look at her. "No," it said. "All monsters must die. The world bathes in evil again and again, no matter how many cleanses are washed through it. Wherever there is evil, there will be a hunter."

"I doh want people to die like that!"

"Hunt with me, child. We must hunt together—that is the way. Angel and human. With the hunter comes the stripping light, the purged souls, the chance for another world to burst forth. All births are full of blood." It looked distracted again, like talking to her was keeping it from something else, like she was taking too long to cooperate. "Not everyone survives."

Bitter was properly scared now. She had *made* this creature, and if it went around killing people, wasn't that the same as if Bitter killed them herself? "Please," she said, "enough people have died. Don't make it worse."

Vengeance's voice softened, and it lowered its head to be level with Bitter's. "Don't worry, child. We will make it better." It sounded like it was trying to be kind, and somehow that made it even more terrifying.

"If you hurt people, it's like I's the one hurting them, don't you see? Because I made you."

Vengeance drew its head back sharply. "You did not *make* me, child. You brought me through." Half of its eyes flickered. "There is a difference." Its smoke rippled. "Time passes. The hunt must begin. Will you come?"

The thought of her creatures existing somewhere else before and without her was a new and unwelcome one. Bitter took a step back, shaking her head. "I—I can't. I can't be part of what you're trying to do."

Vengeance hummed, the sound conveying disappointment with surprising clarity. "So be it. I will seek another hunter."

Bitter opened her mouth to object again, but before she could say anything, Vengeance had poured itself through her window in a long spill, leaving the glass undisturbed. It swirled briefly, then soared off into the sky. Bitter stood by the window, her hands trembling as she watched. She could feel something stretched between them, a connection that ached as it vanished from sight. She sat heavily on her bed, her heart thudding, her arm perfect. The door to her room slammed open, and Blessing rushed in like a memory from another world, her eyes tired and her face smudged with dirt.

"Come on," she said, extending a hand. "It's Eddie."

- - - -

Bitter held tightly to Blessing's hand as they slipped along the side streets into a small park that was filled with people, all holding lit candles. A little kid was handing out marigold garlands, their hands draped in heavy gold flowers. Bitter and Blessing both received garlands and whispered thanks to the child before joining the crowd. Everyone was looking toward a small dais filled with the Assata kids. Bitter gasped when she saw Eddie standing among them, her face bruised and swollen, one dark eye piercing the crowd and a gauze patch covering the empty other. Her body swayed; she must have been on so many painkillers to be able to be out here. Her comrades were thick around her, holding her up. They parted only to let Ube roll his wheelchair to the front. His face was serious, but his mouth was relaxed as he lifted a megaphone to his lips, and his eyes were pools of darkness in the glow of all the candles.

"Thank you all for coming on such short notice," he said, his voice undulating through the air, rich and warm. "We will keep this brief. After many years of fighting, Lucille is speaking with one voice and we will be heard! Tonight the powers that be tried to silence us with force, with their weapons and violence, the only language they speak, the only language they know." A thread of sorrow wound into his words. "We lost one of our own—Chijioke Jackson fell on the front lines today. Eddie DeSantos was injured trying to protect him."

The crowd's gaze swung over to Eddie, who raised a fist, her jaw tight. Someone's arm was firm around her waist. Ube continued, somber and steady. "This war is bloody—we all know this too well. They will not give us our freedom, so we must *take* it! They must understand that Lucille is the people, Lucille is us, Lucille is not a machine that churns out money on the backs of its citizens."

A sharp and short cheer went up from the Assata kids.

"But today we are gathered to take a moment for the costs of this war, the price freedom demands. Chijioke Jackson should be alive. We deserve so much more than what we have been given. We are magnificent beyond measure, we have known more grief than is righteous." His eyes swept over everyone, and Bitter felt a chill cross the back of her neck as tears stung her eyes. "We are here tonight for all the ones we've lost. Join me. For Amadou and Moon, for Carmen—"

Other voices began to chime in, lifting up from in between the ocean of small flames.

". . . Ola and the twins . . ."

". . . Felicity, Helen . . ."

Bitter saw their hands clench around the candles, the marigolds drenching their arms, and she fought back tears alongside them.

". . . Deshaun, Shondra, and their baby . . ."

Ube's voice came back in, rich and rolling. "All of them, they did not die for nothing! We will not let them have died for nothing! We will not stop until all of us are free, until we have torn down what these monsters have built, until we have made a better world—for ourselves, for our children! And when they put one of us in the ground, what then?"

The crowd roared back. "A thousand of us will rise up!"

"We will never stop! And if they make us all angels, each one of us standing here today, fighting here today, then we will be angels!"

This time the crowd's roar made Bitter's eardrums ring. She had never heard so many people so ready to die. Ube's words sent fear skittering through her body. He was calling them angels, and Vengeance's voice echoed in her head. The language would change, it had said, the world would bend. In the distance, she could hear faint sirens.

Blessing tugged at her sleeve. "We need to get out of here *now*."

Bitter didn't move. She was terrified, she was weeping silently, she was entranced by Ube's voice. He was looking over the crowd, somber, his words falling calm and smooth now, spilling over them like dark honey even as the sirens wailed closer and closer.

"*We are each other's harvest*," he said, his voice soft as he recited the Gwendolyn Brooks lines, and the crowd picked it up, their voices a swelling susurrus.

"We are each other's business," they chanted as one. *"We are each other's magnitude and bond."*

Chills raced up Bitter's arms as she watched Ube put down the megaphone. The crowd dispersed like a scattered breath, flames folding into the night. Blessing tugged on Bitter's arm, and Bitter let her best friend pull her out of the park. Marigold petals littered the ground, dropping from their garlands. Bitter wiped tears from her face, following Blessing blindly as they headed back to Eucalyptus. Blessing didn't slow down until they were safely on school grounds, where she sighed with relief and turned to Bitter, taking her hands.

"Eddie's going to be okay," she said. "Aloe texted me and said to check in on you. I thought you'd want to see her for yourself."

Bitter sniffed and nodded. "Thank you," she said.

Blessing pulled her into a hug. "I know it's scary," she whispered, and Bitter almost laughed because Blessing didn't know about Vengeance yet, didn't know what Bitter had done, what Bitter had unleashed into Lucille. There were no words to start explaining it—where would she even begin? With the blood and the little girl inside the lost years?

Bitter wrapped her arms around Blessing and tried not to feel like she was losing her mind because she had made an angel and there was no one she could tell about it because her secret was too old, too big, and now it was going to kill someone. She could feel the panic unwinding inside her, a wild and fraying thread.

"Breathe," Blessing ordered, and Bitter tried to obey, squeezing her eyes shut as she dragged air into her tight lungs.

They were interrupted by Alex's voice, high-pitched and frantic in a way Bitter had never heard it before. "Blessing!" she was yelling, and Bitter looked up in time to see Alex running across the lawn, her eyes wide as she skidded to a stop in front of them. "Blessing, Bitter, y'all have to come right now."

"Babe? What's wrong?" Blessing let go of Bitter, and they exchanged a quick worried look. Alex was never like this. Alex was cool and calm, not harried and . . . frightened?

"Are you okay?" Bitter asked.

Alex shook her head. "My—my workshop," she stuttered. "It's in my workshop. You have to come." She grabbed Blessing's hand and pulled her along. Bitter followed them back to the workshop wing, ducking between the hedges of the outdoor garden. Stone sculptures towered over them as they headed for the entrance. Alex paused at the door, then pushed it open slowly, and the three girls crept into the hallway.

"What's in the workshop?" Blessing whispered.

"You wouldn't believe me if I told you," Alex replied. "I need to know I'm not losing my fucking mind."

They came to her studio door, Alex's face pale in the fluorescent hallway lights as she put her hand on the doorknob. Bitter was beginning to have a really bad feeling about this. It was too many things in one night, and whatever had the power to shake Alex up this much was something she wasn't sure she wanted to see, but it was also too late, because they were already there and Blessing was pushing the door open impatiently. "It can't be that bad, whatever it is," she was saying as she stepped into Alex's workshop. Bitter followed her, and then they both stopped in their tracks. Alex looked over their shoulders.

"Told you," she said. Blessing's jaw had dropped open, and Bitter's heart was racing faster than she thought possible.

Half of Alex's studio was taken up by a winged metal creature pacing back and forth. It swung its face toward them, and its eyes were liquid mercury, rippling in the light as they settled on the girls.

"What the *fuck* is that?" Blessing whispered.

"It *was* a sculpture, and I don't know what I did, but that motherfucker came to life, yo." Alex looked like she was ready to dash out of the door at any moment. "Y'all can see it, right? Like, this shit ain't in my head?"

"I can see it," Bitter answered, her voice soft with shock. Vengeance had kept saying *we* like it wasn't alone, and apparently it wasn't. "Does it talk?"

Both Blessing and Alex turned their heads sharply toward her. "Does it do *what,* now?" Blessing replied, her voice alarmed, just as Alex asked, "How did you know it talks?"

Bitter couldn't stop staring at the creature. "I'm Bitter," she said to it.

It opened a mouth full of needled teeth. "Yes," it said, and its voice was like many voices tightly stitched together. "We know. You are the first gate."

Blessing grabbed hold of Bitter's arm, her fingers digging into the skin. "Bitter? What the fuck is going on?"

"See, it said that gate shit to me too," Alex chimed in. "I have no idea what it's talking about."

The creature glanced out of the floor-to-ceiling workshop windows. "The first gate knows," it said. "The hunt begins."

Bitter closed her eyes for a second as a terrible and certain foreboding washed over her. "Please don't," she whispered. "Please don't kill more people."

Blessing's voice grew shrill. "*What?*"

The creature hummed a low sound. "The world changes when angels return," it said. "All monsters must die."

Bitter could feel hot tears leaking out of her eyes again. How was she supposed to stop this? How many more of them were here? "I don't *want* people to die," she said.

"Full of wants," the creature said. "Blind with want, what does your world *need*?" It looked out of the window again, out to Lucille. "Vengeance calls." It flexed its wings and went translucent, just as Vengeance had in Bitter's room. "The hunt begins."

As the girls looked on in shock, the creature took flight, its body passing through the glass of the windows as if it was nothing, like a ghost. They watched it disappear, and then Bitter took a deep breath and turned to Blessing and Alex.

"I have something to tell you," she said, trying not to sound as nervous as she felt, trying to be brave. There were angels roaming Lucille, hunting the monsters. There was no time for secrets anymore.

CHAPTER 9

- - - - - - - - - -

After Bitter finished telling the girls about her drawings and the blood and Vengeance's arrival, the three of them sat on the floor of Alex's studio. Blessing looked at Bitter with a soft concern.

"How come you never said shit about this? It's been years."

"I know." Bitter ran her hands over her head, then bent her knees so she could rest her forehead against them. "It just feel like it belong to a different world, yuh know?"

Alex turned her hand over to show a cut on her palm. "I slipped with one of my tools just before it came alive. . . ."

"Yeah." Bitter's mouth twisted. "Blood is what they need to come through."

Blessing shuddered. "That's dark."

Alex was frowning. "They said they're angels?"

"They said they're going to kill the monsters," Bitter replied, raising her head. "I's a little more worried about that part of it."

"Is that such a bad idea?" Blessing asked. Bitter and Alex glared at her, and she threw up her hands. "I'm just saying! Can you think of a better way to get rid of a billionaire?"

Alex stared at her girlfriend. "Are you serious, babe?"

"What? Eat the rich, remember? Guillotines? How is this any different?"

Alex shook her head. "We gotta go talk to Assata."

Bitter drew back. "For what?"

"We need help, Bitter. We can't handle this shit on our own."

"Yuh think they going to believe us?" The last thing Bitter wanted was to involve Assata in this. She'd spent so long steering clear of them, even since Aloe, even since her friendship with Eddie. And what was she going to say to Eddie now? *I'm sorry?* That would just be pathetic. She'd summoned Vengeance *for* Eddie—how was she supposed to stand in front of Assata and explain that thanks to her, people were going to die?

Blessing reached out and touched Bitter's arm. "It's going to be okay," she said.

"Ube will believe us," Alex added. "Don't worry."

- - - -

Alex made them turn off their phones before leading them on a dizzying route along Lucille's back streets that ended at a dark doorway. She held her finger up to her lips, then knocked on the door in a rapid pattern, her knuckles ringing off metal. A light turned on from the other side, leaking around the edges, and a distorted voice came through the steel.

"Identification."

Alex rattled off a string of numbers and letters that Bitter couldn't follow. There was a pause, and then the door clicked open. Alex pushed Bitter and Blessing through, glancing around the alley before following them inside. A young child in a flowered shirt and gold overalls closed the door behind them, then hugged Alex's knees.

Alex frowned as she crouched down so the child could see her lips. "Taiwo, why you on door duty? Where are the others?"

Taiwo signed a reply, their hands blurring in the air. Bitter tried to follow, but she didn't know enough sign language to understand.

"That's weird," Alex said, almost to herself.

"What is it?" Blessing asked as Alex dropped a kiss on Taiwo's head and the child ran off.

"They're in seclusion," Alex replied. "But it's all wrong. The timing is off. Something else is going on."

Bitter desperately wanted to ask Alex if the rumors were

true, because it was kinda looking that way now, like Alex had left Assata for Eucalyptus, but she kept her mouth shut and followed as Alex led them down a wide hallway that opened up into a sprawling kitchen. A dark-skinned woman with gray hair and soft wrinkles around her eyes was seated on a low wooden stool, surrounded by a semicircle of young children on cushions and colorful mats. Taiwo was settling back in among them, and the woman was reading Sonia Sanchez out loud to the children, tortoiseshell glasses perched on her nose. A girl with afro puffs was sitting on a stool next to her, signing along as the woman spoke. They broke off as soon as the woman saw Alex. Her bright red lips split into a smile, and she put the book down on her lap, the pages resting on the canary yellow of her dress.

"Baby girl," she said, her voice soft. "It is good to see you."

Alex's eyes lit up, and she smiled at the children as she went over to the woman, bending to touch her feet before being pulled into a tight hug. "It's good to see you too, Miss Bilphena."

Bitter and Blessing stood awkwardly to the side. It felt like they were crashing some sort of family reunion. Miss Bilphena gave them a brief smile, then returned her attention to Alex.

"What you need, baby? Have you eaten?"

"I'm good, Miss Bilphena. We just here to see Ube."

Something flickered in the woman's face. She unfolded from the stool and gestured to one of the older children to come take her place, handing the book to them. "Read for a little bit, baby," she murmured, then jerked her head at Alex, walking over to the far end of the kitchen. Bitter and Blessing followed behind, still unsure of whether they were welcome. Miss Bilphena hadn't said a word to either of them yet, but her face when she turned back to Alex was different, tense and controlled.

"You're bringing outsiders to the safe house, Alex. There better be a good reason."

"Yes, ma'am. It's . . . it's an emergency."

Miss Bilphena looked at Bitter and Blessing, unconvinced. "Then you can tell me what it is."

Alex faltered. Bitter didn't blame her—it would sound unbelievable to say it out loud to anyone who hadn't seen what they'd seen in that studio.

Miss Bilphena folded her arms and raised an eyebrow. "Go on," she said. "If you can say it to Ube, you can say it to me."

Alex bit her lip, and Blessing leaned forward to step in for her girlfriend. "Well, Alex accidentally brought some kind of angel to life, and it's lowkey on a mission to murder a bunch of people in Lucille—not that I'm entirely opposed to that, but I would say that, yeah, it's kind of an emergency."

Bitter took a deep breath and pressed her fingers to her eyes. "Blessing . . . ," she started to say, but when she looked up, Miss Bilphena was staring at them with new alarm.

"We're not lying," Alex said, her voice knotted with worry. "I know it sounds ridiculous, but—"

Miss Bilphena raised her hand for silence, and Alex broke off, shooting a glare at Blessing, who shrugged. Bitter watched the older woman struggle for control again, the muscles in her jaw flexing.

"You can trust them, Alex?" Her eyes were dark and sharp behind her glasses, and Alex almost flinched under her gaze. "And I mean with the lives of those babies in there, because that's what's at stake. You know this."

Alex paled, but she didn't back down. "Yes, ma'am."

Blessing slid her hand into Bitter's and squeezed it tightly. Miss Bilphena stared at them, then hissed out a sharp breath. "Okay," she said. Her alarm hadn't receded, and Bitter realized it had been there all along, even as she'd smiled a calm welcome at Alex when they'd entered. She'd just been masking it, but the woman was scared, terrified even. "There are spirits in the atrium." Her voice was low and frayed.

Alex blinked. "I'm sorry, what?"

"They arrived not long ago. We called an unscheduled seclusion, and I took the children in here before they could see."

Bitter felt a sudden tug in her stomach, a quick discomfort. "Oh no," she said out loud. Vengeance had said it would find another hunter. Where better to look than in Assata? "They're *here*."

Blessing whipped her head around. "See now, I really don't like how you said that. Who's here?"

Bitter listened. The air had a faint buzzing sound to it. She turned to Miss Bilphena. "What did these spirits look like?"

The woman shook her head. "It happened so fast. I could *feel* them, the air got so heavy. Ube told us to get the children out, and Hibiscus called seclusion immediately." She gave a faint smile. "I had to pull it together for the little ones—they pick up on everything."

Alex put a hand on her arm. "Thank you, Miss Bilphena. We've always been lucky to have you."

"Oh, shush." She dabbed at the corners of her eyes. "I gotta get back to the babies."

Alex grimaced. "They're not going to like me interrupting seclusion."

"It's unusual times, my dear. They'll survive." Miss Bilphena glanced at Bitter and Blessing. "It's nice to meet you, dears." She straightened her shoulders and pulled warmth around her like a force field as she headed back to the children.

"Come on," Alex said. "Atrium's this way."

They went through the kitchen into another wide hallway, this one lined with shelves of plants and art. "How large is this place?" Bitter asked.

"The whole block," Alex replied. "But don't tell anyone I told you that."

"The whole *block*?" Blessing laughed. "That's not possible. It's too big to stay hidden."

Alex didn't laugh back. "Not if you got the right people protecting it."

They came to a set of large wooden double doors, and the feeling in Bitter's stomach intensified, almost like she was about to throw up. Alex took a deep breath. "Here goes fuck all," she muttered, then she pulled the doors open. The buzzing in the air redoubled into a high-pitched whine as the doors creaked loudly; then everything dropped into a dead silence. Bitter blinked at the change in light—the atrium was full of glass, a black sky spread out above the domed ceiling. There was grass under their feet, like they'd just stepped into a hidden garden. Fireflies rose through the air, and lamps hung from chains all around the space, spilling a fiery glow between the citrus trees and flowering bushes. About twenty Assata kids were gathered in the center of the atrium around a weeping willow. A boy with two long braids and beaded earrings was posted by the doors, and as soon as the girls walked in, he took one look at them and let out a piercing whistle to alert the others.

"Masks up!" he yelled, pulling the scarf around his neck to cover his nose and mouth, hiding his high cheekbones.

"Yo, chill," Alex said. "It's just me."

"I don't know who the fuck *they* are," the boy shot back. The Assata kids by the weeping willow were pulling up their hoodies and turning away from the doors.

"What's going on?" Bitter asked.

Alex sighed. "They're protecting their identities. From outsiders."

One of them broke off and loped over in long, aggressive strides. He was wearing a black T-shirt, and the cut of his muscles showed under the fabric. He didn't bother covering his face.

"Y'all need to get out," he said. "Now."

Alex rolled her eyes. "Good to see you too, Hibiscus. How you been?"

He glared at her. "We're in seclusion, Alex. You brought strangers to the house? Who even let you through?"

"Miss Bilphena did. You wanna go take it up with her?"

Bitter held her breath as she watched them stare each

other down. When Hibiscus narrowed his eyes but didn't say anything, Alex gave a brief nod. "This is my girlfriend, Blessing, and her best friend, Bitter. We gotta talk to Ube."

"Ube's busy. We're in *seclusion*."

"I know how it works, asshole. You think I'd be here if it wasn't an emergency?"

Hibiscus growled in the back of his throat with frustration, then dropped his hostility, lowering his voice. "Look, Alex, we got a bigger emergency here. It ain't no time for outsiders."

"Yeah, we heard you had some spirits drop by?" Blessing smiled sweetly at Hibiscus, and Alex groaned.

"Angels," Bitter corrected.

Blessing nodded. "Right. Angels."

"Oh, for fuck's sake." Alex glared at them. "Can you let me handle this?"

"You taking too long," Blessing snapped. "We don't have time for all this Assata bullshit."

"Whoa," Hibiscus said, "now hold the fuck up—"

He was interrupted by the smooth, deep voice everyone knew, the one that washed silence in around it.

"What's going on?" Ube asked. He'd rolled up silently, and his face looked drawn with stress. Bitter realized she didn't know how late it was, how long they'd all been up without sleep. She hadn't even been out there; Ube must have been exhausted.

"We got outsiders," Hibiscus complained.

Ube flicked him a look. "Alex isn't an outsider." Hibiscus looked like he wanted to argue that point but decided to hold his tongue. Ube turned to the girls. "What's up?"

Alex folded her arms. "Sounds like we both had some visitors we need to talk about."

Another voice rang out through the atrium, shaking the glass with its dead weight. Bitter felt the ache in her stomach ease up as the sound washed over her. It was Vengeance.

"Let the gates through," it commanded.

Ube tightened his mouth and stared at them for a moment, then spun around to return to the Assata gathering, jerking his head for them to follow. Hibiscus waited for a beat, then walked behind the girls like he was there to contain their presence. As they made their way through the small crowd of Assata kids, Alex raised her hand in greeting, but only a few of them raised theirs in response. The rest just tracked them with suspicious eyes. They were standing in a thick and tight circle, but they parted for Ube as easily as water, opening up right to the center.

Blessing hissed in a breath when they passed through the circle. A handful of figures stood in the middle, shaped like people, but made of nothing like flesh. There was a glimpse of feathers tipped in blood, delicate sheets of fire, metal, and mercury. In the front stood a figure made of smoke, with a scaled head and seven yellow eyes.

"Vengeance," Bitter whispered, shocked to see it outside of the shape she'd painted it in. The angel turned its face to her, eggshells clacking in its neck. It was so terribly foreign in this world, it distorted reality with its presence.

"Child," it said, guttural and deep, "have you come to hunt?"

Ube looked at Bitter, his eyes narrowed, his knuckles tight as he gripped the armrests of his chair. "How do you know it?" he asked, his voice clipped and sharp.

She wilted under his dark gaze. "It's—it's complicated," she managed, her voice thickening around her tongue. There were entirely too many people looking at her.

Ube gave her a smile that didn't have an ounce of amusement in it, like he had more information than he was asking her for. "We gon' have to have a talk about what the *fuck* y'all been doing at Eucalyptus."

Alex flinched at the restrained rage in his voice, but her eyes were locked onto Vengeance, her face pale. "Is that—"

"Yeh, that one's mine," Bitter replied. "It looking real different now, though."

Vengeance tilted its head, and its mouth stretched into an empty, seeping smile. "Touching," it said, its voice thick and grating. "To be claimed."

Bitter took a curious step forward. "Why you shape so?" she asked, gesturing with her hands. "Like a person?"

Vengeance dragged its blank gaze over the gathered Assata kids. "It makes it easier for humans who are not gates."

Blessing stepped closer to Bitter and Alex, taking their hands in hers so the three girls were standing like a chain. "What's going on?" she whispered, fear in her voice. "Is that a monster?"

Vengeance growled so hard and quickly that the room trembled, dust falling from the ceiling.

Hibiscus stepped forward, stretching an arm out to protect the girls. "Cool down," he said to the creature. "They're just asking questions."

It stepped forward. "You are afraid," it said.

Hibiscus swallowed hard. "I'd be a damn fool not to be. But you said you weren't here to hurt us. I want to make sure that doesn't change."

Bitter turned her head. "It said that?"

Ube nodded. "Yeah. It showed up talking some shit about being a hunter and killing monsters, telling us not to be afraid." He looked at Bitter, and his eyes were black

138

accusations. "You said this one is yours, Bitter. It called you a gate? What did you *do*?"

She hadn't even known that he knew her name. Bitter's voice got stuck in her throat. She'd already had to tell her secret to Blessing and Alex—did she have to tell it to this terrifying prophet of a boy too? With nearly all of Assata watching? Eddie wasn't there, and that sent a tendril of worry through Bitter. She hoped her friend was okay.

Ube was waiting for an answer, but Bitter didn't want to open up about the most private part of her life in front of these strangers. On the other hand, Vengeance was there. Vengeance was *there,* in half its force and righteous rage, and she couldn't wish or hope or paint it away, or pretend that it hadn't told her exactly what it was planning to do. Her blood was still a faint brown crust along the edge of its mouth.

"I made a painting," she said to Ube, because that was true, at least.

He glared at her. "*That* is *not* a painting!"

Bitter folded her arms and looked down at her feet. "It's *complicated*," she mumbled. Vengeance had called itself an angel, and so had the creature in Alex's studio, but Bitter was having a hard time accepting that. The woman and man she used to live with had statues of angels all over their house, and they would pray to archangels, even, but all of it was light and ivory robes and pale-skinned men with blond hair gazing blank and benevolent. Angels weren't this, whatever this was. Angels were what Ube had said at the vigil—good people who would die for the revolution, who *had* died for the revolution. Bitter didn't believe that Vengeance being here was bending Lucille all the way down to the language, like it had claimed.

Ube turned back to Vengeance, bravely meeting its yellow gaze. "I'ma ask again," he demanded, and his voice shook only a little. "What are you? Why are you here?"

Vengeance swelled, its shape glitching and losing some form. Smoke leaked out around it. "Child, I have answered. The world changes when the angels return. Show me your monsters. We will hunt them. We will kill them."

Hibiscus looked at Bitter. "It's been talking about monsters since it got here. You got any idea what it means?"

Bitter didn't take her eyes off what she had made. Vengeance's limbs were elongating back to their original length, its body stretching obscenely. Murmurs were breaking out from the rest of the Assata crew, fear growing in their eyes as they watched the creature warp into its first form. "Theron. The police. It wants to . . . get rid of them. The monsters."

Hibiscus raised his eyebrows. "Word? That's not a bad idea."

Blessing elbowed Alex. "See? I'm not the only one who thinks so."

"It wants to *kill* them," Bitter snapped.

Hibiscus seemed unmoved. "Yeah, it's been very clear on that, actually." He didn't look scared. Instead, his eyes were thoughtful as he watched Vengeance expand, the humanoid shape loosening and swelling into the column of smoke Bitter had painted. "Bringing the war to them," he said. "We'd be an army they've never seen before."

Vengeance heard him and snaked its long neck over, yellow eyes glinting. "Yes," it hissed. "A war and an army. The host of righteous fire." The other figures stood back and rustled their forms, spiking the buzz in the air. They looked small next to Vengeance's smoke-filled heft, but Bitter had no desire to see them unfold into whatever their actual shapes were.

Ube came forward, keeping his voice low so the rest of Assata wouldn't hear. "We not tryna start a war," he said.

Hibiscus laughed. "Who you kidding? We already in a war. If these . . . angels have come to give us a hand, I say we take it. What other option is there—to keep throwing ourselves against the city and watching them kill us? How many more deaths will it take, Ube?"

"This is reckless. We don't know what they really are. We don't even know where they came from." Ube's face was tense, his jaw sharp.

Vengeance glanced at him. "We came from the gates," it said. "Eucalyptus leaks divinity. The threshold opens with blood."

Ube looked even more stressed. "What the fuck does that mean?"

Alex grimaced. "It wasn't just Bitter," she said. "I made a sculpture, but I didn't know about the blood. It was an accident."

"That's not the explanation you think it is," Ube snapped.

Bitter stepped in. "They need blood to come through."

Ube's eyes flicked between her and Alex. "These . . . things came through your work?"

Blessing pressed her fingers to the bridge of her nose. "Dammit," she said. "That's why it mentioned Eucalyptus. That's how they're getting here, through everyone's pieces at school."

Vengeance rumbled in its stretched throat, a deep and jagged sound. "Song and story," it said, "blood and anger."

Alex was shaking her head. "That shit ain't possible. You can't get everyone to bleed on their art on the same night! The school would be chaos if that had happened."

"You are human," Vengeance countered. "We can get you to do many things. There are things happening tonight that you know nothing of." It glanced over at Bitter. "Tell them the truth. It is not complicated."

Bitter worried at her lip, feeling the metal of her ring against her teeth. "I called it," she said. "I wanted help. I wanted all this to stop, so I painted it and then I called it through. But I eh know it was going to be like this!"

Ube looked like he was having a hard time processing it all. "And now they want to go on a killing spree."

"Justice," Vengeance corrected.

"I'm not sure murder counts as justice," Bitter shot back.

Vengeance remained unbothered. "Worlds burn when the angels return. All monsters must die."

Hibiscus clapped his hands together. "I'm with it. Let's not keep everyone waiting—they getting stressed out." He turned to the rest of Assata. While Ube spoke like a prophet leading the people, Hibiscus spoke like a soldier who wanted nothing more than to fight.

"*Assata!*" he called out, his voice booming through the atrium, hungry and hot-blooded. It was smoothed into silk, a warrior on a pulpit. Everyone gathered snapped to attention, their eyes fixed on him. "Do not be afraid of these spirits. Our prayers and the prayers of our Elders have been answered! Today we stand with angels among us, come to bring the war to our oppressors, to cut them down with holy fire. We have run from them for too long—tonight we draw the line. To-night they will run from *us*, they will know what fear tastes like, bitter and bloody in the backs of their throats!"

As Hibiscus spoke, Vengeance wrapped itself around him like a wraith, its smoke passing harmlessly through the boy's flesh, so it looked like they had become one terrible thing together. Instead of frightening Hibiscus, it seemed to fortify him. His voice grew even more certain, more steady. "We can *end* this. We can topple those in power out of their seats and reclaim Lucille for the people, at whatever cost. There cannot be one more death, one more person lost in our fight for freedom. Since they will not give us justice, we must take it!"

Vengeance's scaled head snaked high above Hibiscus, its yellow eyes raking over the humans. "Do not be afraid," it said, glitching its voice into the ice-cold charm. "We are here to help you. We are here to protect you. You are the innocent, and we will be your shield. We will hunt together, human and angel. The world will burn, and from its ashes a glorious morning will arise." Some of the Assata kids still looked nervous, but Bitter could see the change happening in a lot of the others, the hope that was awakening in their eyes, because the presence of the angels was an impossible thing, which meant that victory had just become possible, the world had just opened past the stretch of their imaginations. They all wanted this to end, they all wanted to be safe, and now Vengeance and Hibiscus were offering them that in exchange for one vicious hunt.

Bitter slid up to Ube, who was clenching his jaw so hard that it carved his face into sharp lines. "We have to stop this," she whispered. "Before it's too late."

Ube turned to look at her, and she flinched. There was something behind his eyes, something as dark as a lost ocean. "How do you stop an angel?" he asked. He looked out at the faces of the Assata kids, the brightness of hope illuminating them one by one like a spreading fire. "I think we are already too late."

CHAPTER 10

Bitter stared at Ube. "You have to try! They're talking about killing people!"

His face was grim. "I know." Hibiscus was still talking, telling the Assata kids how a new future was finally close enough for them to wrap their hands around. Ube came up next to him, and everyone's eyes shifted over to the boy they knew as their voice in the desert. Hibiscus trailed off into silence, realizing he had lost their attention and Ube hadn't even said a word yet.

A girl in all red with a thick fro piped up. "What do you think, Ube?" she asked. "Are we going to war with these spirits?"

"They're calling themselves angels," Ube replied. "And when they say *hunt,* they mean that they are going to commit murder." He swept his gaze over the group. "My question to y'all is, do you want that blood on your hands?"

"You talking like it's regular people who are going to die,"

Hibiscus interjected. "We're talking monsters. We're talking Dian Theron. You gonna defend that man's life?"

Ube glanced over at him, then made eye contact with Vengeance, who was still wrapped around Hibiscus. "Can you give us some space? This is a human matter."

Vengeance unwound itself from Hibiscus and slithered over to Bitter, settling beside her. "Is this how you humans decide things?" it asked her. "All this talking."

"We take life seriously," she snapped.

"Why?"

Bitter shot a glare at the angel. "What the hell you mean, why?"

"What is a monster's life? How many lives have these monsters taken? How many lives will the hunt save?"

Bitter hesitated. "It doesn't matter if they're monsters," she replied, but there was a fault line in her voice because she did wonder how many people would be safe if people like Theron were just . . . removed.

Vengeance stared at her, seven yellow and unblinking eyes pinning her down. "It should matter."

Hibiscus was facing off with Ube. "You wanna stand here and tell us all that Theron deserves to live? After the shit that man has done? I never thought I'd hear you protect him."

A murmured gasp went up from the Assata kids, and

Ube's eyes turned to black coals. "You really wanna go there with me, Hibiscus?"

Blessing leaned over to Alex. "What's going on?" she whispered. "This shit just got mad tense."

Alex looked as shocked as the others, but she shushed Blessing with a quick hand over her girlfriend's mouth. "Not now," she whispered back.

"I'm just saying!" Hibiscus looked unrepentant. "Your mom would still be here today if she hadn't worked for Theron. If he didn't cut their health care and stick them all in those damn warehouses. Now you saying we shouldn't take him out?"

Ube's voice was a thin blade slicing from his tongue— even the air drew away from the sharp edge. "First of all, keep my mama out your mouth," he said.

Most of the Assata kids murmured in agreement. "That was out of order, Hibiscus," one of them said.

"Yeah, man. Not cool," another echoed.

Hibiscus raised his hands. "My bad. I overstepped."

Ube kept talking. "Second of all, none of us have the right to decide when to end another person's life! That is not justice."

The girl in red frowned. "But, Ube, they decide that all the time with us. Chijioke is *dead* because they decided."

"That's what I'm saying." Hibiscus gestured to the doors of the atrium, to the rest of the safe house. "Those babies in there, do we keep doing this until it's them being shot in the streets? We supposed to be making a better world for them, where they can feel loved and cherished, and how we gon' do that when all we doing is dying? What are we gonna tell them—that literal angels came down to help us win this battle, but we *refused*?"

"Yeah, man." The boy with long braids had left his post by the doors to join the group. "This shit isn't even about justice anymore—it's about survival. Either we die or they die."

Ube raised an eyebrow. "Oh, so you ready to kill folk now, huh? You feeling that froggy?"

Vengeance's voice rumbled through the space. "The angels kill the monsters. Let the blood be on us."

Ube lifted his hand without looking back at Vengeance. "We not talking to you yet," he said, flat and hard.

"Look, it's not like we're the ones doing this," Hibiscus said. "I wouldn't be pitching some shit as wild as this, you know that. But we can't ignore that these creatures showed up in our world with a mission that they sound pretty certain of carrying out. All I'm saying is, the tide is turning in our favor. Why can't we ride the wave into a better future?"

Alex raised her hand. "Well, first of all, the wave is made of blood."

Hibiscus whipped his head around and snarled at her. "*So what?* How much of our blood has been spilled on Lucille's streets? Is their blood worth keeping inside their bodies while ours is not?" His eyes were burning with rage. "I say it is enough! The angels say it is enough!"

Ube reached out and placed a hand on his arm. "Hibiscus—"

"No!" He shook off Ube's hand, furious tears wet on his cheeks. "They are *killing* us, and they won't stop! I'm done arguing with y'all about this shit. I'm with the angels. We're gonna hunt these motherfuckers down, and y'all can be part of making our world safer or you can sit here and bitch about the ethics of stopping murderers." Hibiscus turned to Vengeance, his face set. "Tell me what I need to do."

The angel looked down at him and stretched its mouth into that terrible smile. "Welcome, little hunter," it said, then it looked at the rest of the Assata kids. "Who else hunts with us?"

The girl in red and the boy with long braids glanced at each other, a silent exchange passing between them before they both stepped forward. "We'll hunt," she said, then glanced apologetically at Ube. "For Chijioke."

"And Eddie," the boy added. "For everyone we literally just acknowledged at the vigil."

Ube didn't say anything, but he looked so lonely sitting there as more and more of the Assata kids stepped forward to join Hibiscus and the angels. Bitter wanted to speak up, but she knew she had no right to, not in this space, not even though she'd painted Vengeance into existence, called it into being, and set off this whole cascade. Assata lived in a different world, one of blood and death and unlikely hope, and that was the world the angels had come for. Bitter was just the gate, someone on the border. Who was she to tell them not to seek justice for everyone who had been lost, especially when this looked like the only way justice was ever going to be served? It felt heavy, inevitable, like an avalanche with an old grudge. None of this felt right, but everything that was happening in Lucille was so wrong in the first place that it skewed reality sideways. Was it even possible to make the right choice under these conditions? Assata just wanted the people to be safe, and so did Bitter, and even though she had an unpleasant feeling that the angels weren't the saviors they claimed to be, she also had nothing else to offer, so what was there to say? Nothing.

Blessing came up next to Bitter and slid an arm around her. "It's going to be okay," she said. Bitter dragged in a deep breath as they watched Assata splinter before their eyes, two-thirds of the group going with Hibiscus while the last third hung back.

"This is not good," Alex muttered, folding her arms. Ube

was speaking softly with the Assata kids who chose not to hunt, and those who had volunteered were now gathering around Hibiscus and Vengeance.

"We hunt together," Vengeance was saying. "Human and angel."

The other creatures came forward, still holding their compressed forms, false humanoid shapes that did little to reassure. Alex's angel was still metal, slippery and reflective with mercury eyes. "Do not be afraid," it said.

The girl in red braced herself and stepped closer to it. "I'm not," she answered.

Vengeance smiled emptily. "Good." Bitter watched as it matched up the rest of the angels with the Assata kids, forming small hunting packs.

"Where are you going to go?" she asked, and Vengeance swiveled its long neck in her direction.

"That is for the hunters," it said. "You can still join us, child."

She shook her head. "I don't want to watch people die, even if they are monsters."

A few feet away, Blessing let out a little scream and jumped back as one of the other angels vanished from the atrium, taking along the Assata kids it had been matched with. They blinked out of the air like a dream, leaving gasps and shocked faces in their wake.

Alex's eyes were wide as she poked Bitter's arm. "They can do that?!"

Bitter was just as startled as everyone else. "Apparently so."

Vengeance hummed an amused sound. "We travel for the hunt," it explained. "Through time and space. The humans will be safe."

The rest of the Assata volunteers took deep breaths as the angels reached out and touched them, vanishing in a silent breath, blank air where they once were.

Ube looked distraught. "I'm going to check on the children," he said, turning away from the disappearings. The Assata kids who chose to stay behind gathered around him to leave as well, and Hibiscus looked on but said nothing. It was Vengeance who broke the thick and sudden silence, its cool voice slithering through the atrium as it snaked its neck toward Ube.

"Would you like to be healed, child?"

Ube stared back at the angel, his face blank. "What?"

Vengeance reached a long smoky limb out to the boy, yellow eyes intent. "So you may walk."

Bitter could almost feel Alex's hackles rise as she took a step toward the angel, her fists tight. Ube flinched and moved away from Vengeance's reach. "No!" he said. "Why would you even ask that?"

Alex cut in sharply. "There is nothing wrong with Ube,"

she said, and the rest of the Assata kids murmured in agreement, even Hibiscus.

The angel's eyes flickered between the humans. It seemed confused. "He does not wish to be whole?"

Blessing put her hand to her mouth, aghast. The air in the room was sharp now, tense. Alex took a deep, furious breath, but Ube shook his head slightly at her and swiveled his chair around, bringing himself up to the angel. Vengeance towered above him, inhuman and terrifying, but Ube's face was calm. When he spoke, his voice rolled through the space like the night sky was pulled out of his mouth, strong and certain.

"I am not broken," he said. "I am already whole."

Vengeance swooped its long neck down, bringing its face level with Ube's. Bitter felt a pang of anxiety. Was it going to hurt Ube for disagreeing? Was it going to ignore him and do whatever it wanted to his body anyway? She could still remember the almost unbearable heat that had flushed through her arm when Vengeance had healed her cut, back in her room. What would that feel like for Ube—like being burned alive?

Ube wasn't backing down, not even with the angel's many eyes fixed intently on him. "I am already whole," he repeated, his voice softer, more intimate, as if he was telling Vengeance a secret. A taut moment of silence passed before Vengeance reared back and up, its smoke glitching.

"Yes," it said. "I understand now." It regarded Ube thoughtfully. "You humans are . . . unpredictable."

"We're human," Ube snapped. "And I think it's time for you to leave."

Vengeance swept its eyes across the room, resting briefly on Bitter. "The hunt calls," it said. "We will see you."

It drifted up to Hibiscus and placed a claw on his shoulder, the tip of it sinking through him. Hibiscus shuddered like he'd been touched by a ghost, but he didn't step away. He glanced at Ube, and his face wavered with a shadow of fear. "I'm sorry," he said. The branches of the weeping willow hung mournfully above them.

"Do what you gotta do," Ube replied, his voice bitter and resigned. He turned to follow the remaining Assata kids out of the atrium. Vengeance vanished with Hibiscus, the last of the hunters, and Bitter stood there with Alex and Blessing, almost alone under the dark sky.

"What do we do now?" Blessing asked, her voice unsure.

Alex put an arm around her girlfriend. "We'll figure it out."

Ube paused at the wooden doors and glanced back at them. "Y'all coming or what?" A streak of relief ran through Bitter. If Assata wasn't kicking them out of the safe house yet, then this whole situation felt less alone, like maybe Alex was right and they really could figure it out, find a way to undo this thing she'd done by bringing Vengeance through. The invitation in Ube's voice felt like a chance, and as Alex pulled her and Blessing along to catch up with the others, Bitter allowed herself to hope that this wouldn't end entirely in blood.

CHAPTER 11

The lights were dimmed in the kitchen as they walked into it, and all the little children were gone. Miss Bilphena stood watering an enormous monstera plant that vined over the kitchen window, and a sky-blue kettle whistled on the stove. "Get that for me, baby," she said without turning around, and three of the Assata kids moved toward the kettle as one body.

"We lost folks to the angels," Ube said. In Miss Bilphena's presence, he seemed young again, tired and scared.

She put down her watering can and wiped her hands on her dress before walking up to Ube and placing a hand against his cheek. "We'll have some tea in the den and you can tell me all about it," she said, as if debriefing after a visit from angels was normal. It seemed as if having the angels physically out of the house had lifted her fear away, and now she could focus on the distressed young people in front of her instead of terrifying unknowns lurking in the atrium. Tenderness radiated from Miss Bilphena like warm light stealing through the room. Bitter could feel all the Assata kids turn to it like new leaves to the sun, relief dropping their shoulders and loosening their necks.

"Y'all grab your mugs and show the new kids where the tea cabinet is," Miss Bilphena said. "Ube and I are going to go on ahead and have a little chat. We'll have our usual." She left with her hand resting lightly on his shoulder, and Bitter watched as Alex merged seamlessly in with the rest of the group, as if she'd never left. They passed each other bright ceramic mugs from the rustic wood shelves on the kitchen wall, seeming relieved to be doing something normal, something that didn't require thinking about vanishing angels and wars and impending bloodshed. Alex beckoned to Bitter and Blessing as she pulled open a cabinet door.

"Okay, so this is where all the tea is kept," she said, and Blessing whistled. It was a ridiculous amount of tea, in jars and muslin bags, handwritten labels scribbled and hanging from small tags. "Miss Bilphena drinks ginger with honey—"

"I got her mug over here," a kid with locs and a snakebite piercing called out. "Someone pass me the honey?" A jar of manuka honey went from hand to hand, and Alex added a tea bag full of dried ginger.

"Ube drinks . . ." Alex paused and frowned. "Does he still drink peppermint?"

Another girl reached over her shoulder and grabbed a jar. "Yup, I got it."

"Bet." Alex took down a box and turned it over to read the label. "I think you'll like this one, Blessing. It's hibiscus with blood orange."

"Ooh, I want that too," Bitter piped up. They stepped away from the cabinet to let everyone else make their picks, then filled up their mugs with hot water, watching the tea bags swell and float.

"Tea is kind of a house ritual," Alex explained as she led them down the hall and around the corner into the den. "Everyone gathers in the den and we take a minute to just . . . sit with each other."

Bitter could feel exhaustion sneaking through her, a combination of the warm tea cupped in her hands and the coziness of the den. The large room was full of pillows and cushions, oversized beanbag chairs that you could sink into, deep couches low to the ground. It made Bitter want to curl up and just rest for a moment—it felt safe enough to, even though she'd never been there before. The feeling took her by surprise. New places often had her on alert, spiky for weeks before she'd settle down, remnants of the lost years inside the foster homes. Even her own room at Eucalyptus had been hard to settle into, until one evening when Miss

Virtue had stopped by, about a week after Bitter had arrived. Her gray hair flared out wild and curly from her scalp, and she was wearing a purple suit the color of smashed berries. She'd knocked politely, waited till Bitter invited her in, then looked around at the room.

"It's a little sparse, isn't it?" she'd said to Bitter, and Bitter had shrugged. Putting down roots was dangerous, and Eucalyptus had been so new then, it hadn't felt like home. Miss Virtue had walked up and looked at Bitter with those ghostly gray eyes of hers gleaming out from her dark face. Bitter remembered feeling both seen and pinned by that gaze, uncomfortably so. "We will never cast you aside," Miss Virtue had said, and something about her voice seemed to reverberate through Bitter's room, like it was layering over itself, like it was a spell. "You will always have this room, come hell or high water." She had said it with such grim certainty that it felt more like a prophecy than a reassurance, and Bitter could feel the surety of it brush against her bones. She had just nodded, unable to speak, and Miss Virtue had nodded back, then left. It still took Bitter a while to accept Eucalyptus as home, but Miss Virtue's proclamation was a big part of that, burned into her memory and echoing on the nights when panic shook Bitter awake and gasping.

There was something about the Assata safe house that reminded Bitter of Eucalyptus and Miss Virtue, that spirit of a space that was designed for the lost ones, the abandoned ones, designed to hold them safe and tell them they never had to leave again. Bitter hadn't expected to find this same vibe here, to find actual tenderness within Assata. She'd thought they were just about fighting on the front lines, that their home space would be full of loud debates and decrying, but instead it was simply a bunch of tired kids climbing onto soft furniture, holding their mugs of tea and telling Miss Bilphena what had happened in the atrium with the angels. Bitter joined Alex and Blessing on a corduroy couch, tucking herself against the arm like she was back in her room.

Blessing snuggled in next to her. "You okay?" she asked.

Bitter nodded. "It just a lot."

"She's the one who called the angels out," the snakebite kid was saying, pointing straight at Bitter, who flinched as everyone's eyes swung to her.

"Why *did* you call them?" Miss Bilphena asked gently.

Bitter drew her knees up into her chest and looked down at her feet. She felt like bursting into tears. "They hurt Eddie," she managed to say, and her voice cracked on her friend's name. "I just wanted them to stop hurting people."

Alex reached over and put a hand on Bitter's shoulder. "It's okay, B."

Bitter shook her head, wiping tears out of her eyes. "It's

not. They're just going to hurt more people, and it's my fault. I'm so sorry I started all this." The silence in the den was heavy, and she was afraid to see what was in the Assata kids' eyes, but Bitter still forced herself to look up. To her surprise, they were all staring at her without any animosity, with some warmth even.

"You did all that for Eddie?" Ube asked, and Bitter nodded.

"I eh mean for it to go this far. I was just really angry, and then Vengeance showed up. I eh know the other ones would come too."

"It's all good." Ube gave her a small smile. "Thank you for trying."

His kindness just made Bitter want to cry even harder, but she choked it back and nodded, sinking deeper into the couch.

"D'you wanna go see Eddie?" he asked, and Bitter's heart leaped.

"I can see her?"

A familiar voice interrupted, startling her. "Actually, she's sleeping now." Aloe was standing in the doorway with his arms folded, his face stony.

A small shock ran through Bitter as she realized that with everything going on with the angels, she'd completely forgotten to wonder where Aloe was in all of this, ever since he'd left to drop off supplies for Eddie. Had he been at the safe house when the angels arrived? How much had he heard of what the others had just shared with Miss Bilphena?

Aloe's eyes fixed on hers. "Can we talk out here for a minute, Bitter?"

She nodded and climbed off the couch, trying to ignore how awkward she felt. She could tell that Aloe was upset, but she couldn't figure out why. They stepped out of the den, and he walked down the hall a little, then stopped. "Were you even going to tell me you were here?" he asked.

Bitter looked down. "I forgot," she said. "There was so much going on—"

"With the angels. I know." A corner of Aloe's mouth quirked as Bitter glanced up at him in surprise. "What, you thought I'd be as out of the loop as you kept me?"

"No, that's not what I meant."

"Isn't it? You literally told everyone else about it before you told me. You didn't call, didn't answer any of my messages, nothing. And don't tell me you're bad with your phone this time."

Bitter patted down her clothes, realizing that she didn't even have her phone on her. "I must have left it at Eucalyptus." She took a step toward Aloe. "I'm sorry you feel left out—"

He barked out a laugh and shook his head. "You don't even get it."

"How you find out about the angels?"

"What, you mean the angels you apparently called out and didn't bother telling me about? I was here when they arrived, and one of the other kids updated me after they left. I couldn't enter the seclusion because I'm not Assata, so I stayed with Eddie." A small but bright resentment burned in his eyes. "Somehow you got into seclusion, though. I thought you didn't even fuck with Assata, but I guess you get privileges for setting all this off in the first place."

Bitter felt a tendril of anger curl through her. "Yuh think I'm lucky to be in the middle of this shitstorm?"

Aloe shrugged. "You seem real comfortable here for someone who was talking shit about Assata the whole time."

She didn't understand why he was angry. "Aloe, you upset because I eh tell you about the angels or because Assata gave me access, which one? Blessing and I came here with Alex, and we involved in this angel business. That's the only reason Ube let us into their seclusion thing."

"That's exactly my point!" Aloe burst out. "You started this whole angel thing, and fine you didn't tell me because it's a big deal and you turned to your girls like I'm not part of your crew, but we can talk about that later. But whether you like it or not, you *are* at the center of this, and that's what got you into Assata, and you don't even *care*. You don't want to hunt, you don't want to be part of it, and it's not fair, because

164

I've been out there with them on the front lines, I'm the one who patches them up, and I didn't even get a chance to decide if I wanted to go with the angels!"

Too many thoughts were crowding Bitter's mind, noisy and overlapping. "I never knew you felt left out by Assata. You could have joined them if you wanted to," she heard herself saying. "Who holding you back from it?"

Aloe stared at her incredulously. "I want to make art, Bitter. I *want* to be at Eucalyptus, with you. I don't think that means I should have to choose between Eucalyptus and Assata or be cut out from shit like this as if I'm not part of their community. What if they get hurt on the hunt?"

"It's fine—the angels can heal. They doh need you." Bitter spoke quickly, trying to reassure Aloe, so she didn't realize what she'd said until she heard it out in the air and saw his eyes go stony. She clapped her hands over her mouth. "Wait, no—"

Aloe's jaw was tight. "No, it's fine. You said what you meant."

How could they be having their first fight in the middle of this? Bitter had never seen this side of Aloe, where he sounded not just jealous but sour. It felt like the angels' arrival had shaken something loose in their relationship, and Bitter couldn't understand it. "I just want you to be safe, Aloe. Why you vexing over this? It doh sound like you."

Aloe gave a brief and empty laugh, then ran his hand over his short locs. "I just want to be helping people, Bitter. I don't think you understand how important that is to me. I would have gone with the hunters, and to be very honest, I get that you don't like doing frontline shit, but I don't understand how you can just stay behind."

Bitter drew back from the accusation in his voice, even though she could tell that he'd said it as gently as he could. "I dare you to go and say that to Ube," she snapped, her voice tight. "He chose to stay behind too, but I eh see you lashing out at him just because you didn't get to go watch people get killed."

"Ube didn't call the angels through," Aloe shot back, ignoring the last part of her jab. "*You* did. You really don't see how this is your responsibility? Bitter, you didn't talk to anyone, you didn't call us. I didn't even know you could do shit like this! And now I'm finding out all these . . . these *secrets* about you. Like, what the fuck, B? How are we together and I'm the *last* person to be looped in?"

Bitter stared at him in shock. She hadn't been keeping secrets from him—the things she drew and what happened with them couldn't be secrets if they were only real in her world. Aloe was part of another world, with Blessing and Alex and Eucalyptus, and Bitter had never planned for the two worlds to collide so disastrously. She could see the hurt steeping behind Aloe's eyes and she wanted to make it better, but it also seemed so trivial in the face of what Vengeance and the other angels were about to do. Aloe didn't understand. He hadn't been there—he'd never seen Vengeance in its full and unfurled form. All he had to work with were the secondhand accounts he'd overheard from the Assata kids in the den, and Bitter didn't know how to tell him that this was so, so much worse than he could imagine. It was bigger than his feelings; it was bigger than *her* feelings, and she was the one who would have to reckon with the truth of what he'd said. She had called the angels through. If they couldn't be stopped, that was blood on her hands, and Bitter had no idea how she could stay sane after something like that. She wasn't Assata—she hadn't been prepared for frontline costs.

Aloe was staring at her like he was waiting for her to say something that would stitch it all back together. Bitter felt beyond empty. The space between them was a canyon crammed into a hallway. She opened her mouth, but nothing came out, because there was nothing she could say that would make Aloe feel better and also be true. He hadn't been a priority in the last few hours, and he wouldn't understand why, because he didn't understand what her life had suddenly been warped into.

"Everything okay out here?" Miss Bilphena had joined

them in the hallway, her voice low but firm. "You two were getting a little loud."

Bitter and Aloe both looked down at their feet, rolls of sullen energy pouring off them, but they didn't say anything. Miss Bilphena looked them over for a moment. Then her face gentled. "It's been a very long day," she said. "Do you have any idea how late it is?"

Bitter was clueless. It felt like time had muddled itself into a dark, soupy stretch of heartbreak and terror.

Miss Bilphena shook her head. "You both need to get some sleep. Be gentle with yourselves and your bodies."

"How can we sleep when there are *angels* out there?" Aloe asked, his hands tightening into fists. "As if everything's okay and nothing's happening!"

Miss Bilphena went up to him and took one of his clenched hands in hers. "Breathe, Aloe." He inhaled shakily, and his fingers uncurled as he exhaled. "In order to fight, we must know when to rest," she continued. "Even getting a few hours of sleep makes a huge difference. We'll gather again in the morning and discuss next steps, don't worry. I'm going to call more of the Elders in, and we'll see what can be done."

"What if they kill someone tonight?" Bitter asked, her fingers twisting together. She could see Vengeance's mouth stretching open like a nightmare, coated in her own blood. "Shouldn't we be stopping them instead of resting?"

Miss Bilphena sighed. "There is nothing more we can do tonight, baby. We don't have enough information. I know it's hard, but for now, it is out of our hands." She waited for Bitter to nod, then turned back to Aloe. "Take her upstairs to the tangerine room."

Bitter wasn't sure about spending the night in the Assata safe house. She wanted her room, her paintings surrounding her like a siege wall. "Wouldn't we be better protected at Eucalyptus?" she asked. "No offense, Miss Bilphena."

The older woman laughed. "Not at all. I know you used to the walls of your school, but rest assured, our safe house is impenetrable, baby girl. We have more to protect within these walls than Eucalyptus does. Those who are out hunting now know only too well what it is like to be hunted."

"Impenetrable?" It was a bold claim, as far as Bitter was concerned. Eucalyptus was safe because it wasn't considered a threat, so how could Assata assure that they were just as safe?

Miss Bilphena winked. "We have our secrets. Some tech, some spirit work, and no one can find or touch us."

Bitter frowned. "You joking," she complained.

"No, she's talking about Sunflower," Aloe said. "She's been in charge of their security for decades."

"Oh, she's an Elder?"

Both Aloe and Miss Bilphena made the same face, their noses scrunching up. "Sunflower doesn't work within time like the rest of us," Miss Bilphena said delicately. "Think of her as . . . ageless."

"Eddie once told me to think of her as a cyborg," Aloe said, a small smile on his face. "Like she's a person, a spirit, and tech all fused together. No one knows how she works, but she works. Keeps the safe house masked at all times, on all fronts."

Bitter side-eyed him. "The tech part I does understand, but . . . spirit work? Come on, nuh."

Miss Bilphena raised an eyebrow. "Coming from the girl who called an angel out of a painting?"

Bitter flushed.

"Exactly." Miss Bilphena's voice slid into the cadence of a teacher, clearly a role she'd spent most of her life in. "We've known that the other realms are real for a long time. We've called on them for centuries, for millennia, since and before our ancestors were taken over the deep water. We can ask spirit for shielding and protection, and in this case, to keep the safe house unseen in the eyes of Lucille. Sunflower has been masking the house for more years than even I know. Trust me, child, it cannot be breached."

"Except by angels," Aloe pointed out.

Miss Bilphena laughed. "Well, they are a clear exception. A shocking one, obviously. We've never had the other side reach over so blatantly, but it makes sense." She flapped her hands at them. "That's enough talk. Off to bed with both of you—rest your angry little tongues."

Bitter watched as she sailed back into the den, then glanced over at Aloe. "You still vex?" she asked.

He sighed and shook his head. "Yes and no. It's just—it's been a really bad day."

Bitter worked up her nerve to reach out and pull him into a warm hug. Aloe was always the one doing the comforting—it hadn't really occurred to her that maybe he just needed what he always gave so freely. "I real sorry my communication was shit today," she said as he slowly wrapped his arms around her. "It will make more sense after you see the angels. Just know I never meant to hurt you or leave you out, okay?"

He pressed his lips to her head, and Bitter felt the knots in her heart ease up a little. "I'm sorry I was lashing out at you," he whispered. "I didn't realize how much it stung not being a full part of Assata until you got involved in it, but I shouldn't have taken it out on you. I'm so glad you're safe. Me, I can't imagine what I'd do if something happened to you."

Bitter squeezed him tightly. "Same," she said. He was whole under her hands, and they were together and safe for now. The day could have gone very differently. "How's Eddie?" she asked.

"Not talking much. She wasn't even here when I arrived. Turns out she decided to go to the vigil instead of resting. I had to patch up a few of the others while waiting for her to come back."

Bitter leaned her cheek against his shoulder. "Blessing took me to the vigil. I was shocked that Eddie was up and about."

"Yeah, she definitely should have been in bed. But she said she wanted to show up for Chijioke, and she wanted to remind people what had been done to her while it was still fresh, you know? Sounds brutal, but she said it was—what's the word she used? Effective."

Bitter winced. "She shouldn't have had to do that." She could still see of Eddie up on that dais, her face swollen past recognition.

"There are a lot of things we shouldn't have to do," Aloe said, and his voice sounded sad. "That's why half of Assata is out hunting with the angels. They're doing what none of us should have to do."

Bitter didn't want to argue. They could both agree that the world wasn't supposed to be like this. For tonight, that had to be enough.

"Come on," Aloe said, guiding her upstairs. The walls of the staircase were lined with handmade quilts, carefully stitched words and pictures. Bitter trailed her fingers across them lightly. "These are beautiful," she said.

"Remind me to ask Miss Bilphena to tell you about them another time," Aloe said. "You'll love the story." He took her to the tangerine room, which was covered in citrusy wallpaper, rich painted fruit heaping from green stems.

"Oh, it's literally the tangerine room." Bitter laughed. It was small but cozy, with a large bed taking up most of the floor space. Aloe lay on top of the covers and reached his arms out to her.

"Come and rest for a bit," he said.

Bitter was only too happy to climb up and snuggle against his chest. His fingers stroked along her spine in gentle lines, and she could feel his ribs expanding and contracting under her cheek. She'd thought it would be impossible to sleep, but in his arms and within the walls of Assata, Bitter was surprised to find exhaustion catching up with her, severing her from the awake world. She didn't know if she believed in the spirit stuff Miss Bilphena had been talking about, but clearly everyone else did, so just in case it was real, Bitter said a quick prayer that she would wake up to a world different from the one she was drifting out of.

CHAPTER 12

The next morning, Lucille was on fire.

Bitter woke up to the acrid smell of smoke seeping through the window. Aloe was already sitting up in bed, sleepy and alarmed. "What's going on?" he asked. "What's burning?"

Muffled shouts came from down the hallway, along with quick footsteps as someone ran past, banging on the doors. Their door was flung open, and Alex looked in. "Oh, good," she said, breathless. "You're already awake."

"W'happening?" Bitter asked, sitting up. Her head felt foggy.

"There's been a breach of the safe house," Alex replied.

"What?" Aloe's voice pitched high as he jumped out of bed. "But that's impossible."

"I know." It was difficult to read Alex's expression. "We got an outsider, and Miss Bilphena wants y'all down in the kitchen."

Bitter felt a flutter of panic start in her. One night out-side Eucalyptus and this happened. She should have never listened to Miss Bilphena's promises about the Assata house being impossible to break into. Still, it was strange—Alex didn't look as alarmed as Bitter felt. That didn't match up if someone had really broken into what was supposed to be an impenetrable safe house. Bitter frowned. "You sure is us she want? Shouldn't we stay in here until allyuh . . . contain the threat, or whatever?"

Alex made a face. "Yeah, so we're not entirely sure that the breach is a threat."

"That doh make no sense, Alex."

"Ugh." Alex sighed. "It's Miss Virtue, okay? The breach is Miss Virtue."

Bitter swung her legs off the bed, shocked. "Miss Virtue? *Our* Miss Virtue?"

"Yup. She just . . . walked right into the house and made herself a cup of tea. Was waiting in the kitchen for half an hour before one of the lookouts noticed her."

"Like I said," Aloe reemphasized, "that's *impossible*. You know that, Alex."

"I mean, yeah, I know, but clearly someone didn't loop Miss Virtue in! She saying she's here for the Eucalyptus kids."

Bitter pulled on her shoes. "To take us back? It not against

the rules to have sleepovers, or is it because we're with Assata specifically?"

"Some sleepover this is," Aloe muttered, and Bitter shot
him a glare.

"Look, I don't know shit about what's going on," Alex replied. "All I know is that everyone's freaking out because this
has literally never happened—they're sending someone up
to the roof to get Sunflower, and Miss Bilphena wants us in
the kitchen. Dassit. Can we go now?"

It didn't make any sense, no matter how hard Bitter tried
to think about it as she and Aloe followed Alex downstairs.
How could Miss Virtue have snuck in? *Why* would Miss Virtue have snuck in? An unpleasant dread rolled around Bitter's stomach, and she prayed desperately that this didn't
have anything to do with Vengeance. It was impossible.
What would Miss Virtue know about angels or the things
that had burst out of her students' work in the indigo thick
of the past night? Then again, it had always seemed like Miss
Virtue knew everything about Eucalyptus and everyone who
lived there, everyone she protected.

When they got to the kitchen, Miss Virtue was indeed
sitting at the table in a white snakeskin suit with matching
boots. Her face was calm and almost pleasant, but her gray
eyes looked slightly feral. She was sipping tea from a delicate

china cup, and Miss Bilphena was sitting across from her, wrapped in a silk robe with her hair cascading around her shoulders. They made a gorgeous if unlikely picture together. They were also surrounded by a squad of Assata kids who were armed with machetes and seemed determined to not let Miss Virtue step a hair out of place.

Miss Virtue smiled when she saw her Eucalyptus kids walk in. "Good morning, darlings," she said. "The city is burning—have you noticed?"

Bitter blinked, unsure of what to say. Blessing was sitting on one of the counters, her legs swinging and her face studiously blank. Ube was making some toast as if anything about that morning was normal.

"What are you doing here?" Aloe blurted out, and Miss Bilphena raised an eyebrow as she drank some of her tea.

"An excellent question," she agreed. "I've been waiting for Virtue to give us some clarity about this . . . unexpected situation."

Bitter folded her arms and glared at Miss Bilphena. "Yeah, I thought allyuh said this house was safe, that no one could break in. Or was that just a lie?"

About half of the machetes swung in her direction as the Assata kids shifted their unfriendly stares to her.

"Did you just call Miss Bilphena a liar?" Ube asked,

spreading blueberry jam on his toast, not even looking at them. "I'd take that back if I was you. Especially in this house."

Bitter raised her hands. "I was just asking! Alex said there's a breach, and you said a breach was impossible, so what the hell?"

Miss Bilphena gestured at the machetes, and they swung back to Miss Virtue, who sighed and placed her cup on its porcelain saucer with a small clink.

"Bilphena, is this really necessary? Your children are a little"—she waved her hand vaguely around—"knife-happy, don't you think?"

"They're understandably distressed, Virtue. You have no business being here."

"I beg to disagree. My students are nothing if not my business."

Ube bit into his toast with a loud crunch. "They're not allowed to visit Assata?"

Miss Virtue scalded them all with one dragging look. "No, what I tend to frown upon is when they call angels through into Lucille en masse." Her voice was a razor blade made of ice, and it froze the air in the kitchen immediately.

Bitter's stomach dropped. "How do you know about that?"

"Darling." Miss Virtue crossed her legs and leaned back in her chair. "I think we've got bigger problems than that, don't you?"

Ube had stopped midchew, slowly processing her words. "Did she just say *angels*?"

"Yes," Miss Bilphena bit out. "And again, what I would like is some *clarity*, Virtue."

"Oh, for goodness' sake." Miss Virtue stood up, and all the machetes moved a few inches closer as the Assata kids stepped forward, raising their blades to shoulder height. Miss Virtue looked down at them and narrowed her eyes. "Bilphena, call your puppies to heel."

Ube came forward and tossed his half-eaten toast on the table. "Y'all chill," he ordered. Half of them tried to protest, but he wasn't having it. "I said chill. Is she even armed?"

"We haven't got a chance to pat her down."

Miss Virtue smiled without any humor. "They value their hands staying attached to their arms, you see."

"Virtue, they are children!" Miss Bilphena said, shocked.

"*Armed* children. I like to keep that distinction clear, thank you."

"Machetes down," Ube insisted. "If she got into the house and through all of Sunflower's wards without being detected, I don't think those are going to do any good."

Miss Virtue gave him an appraising look. "I see the stories are true. You *are* wise, little one."

Ube bristled at the diminutive, but any objection he was about to voice faded away when the rest of the Assata kids shifted their gazes to the doorway and immediately lowered their weapons, stepping back as far as the room would let them. Miss Bilphena followed their stares and let out a tight smile.

"So nice of you to join us, Sunflower."

Bitter whipped her head around. A woman stepped into the kitchen soundlessly, wearing glistening black sandals and a crisp midnight agbada that cascaded off her shoulders, its folds draped with a casual elegance. It was embroidered with shimmering thread, as if electricity ran through the fabric. The woman glanced at Miss Bilphena but didn't respond to her welcome, shifting her eyes to assess Miss Virtue instead. Bitter couldn't stop staring. Sunflower's head was shaved bald, smooth dark skin wrapping around her skull. Her earlobes were thick with clusters of diamonds, tracking all the way to the tops of her ears and casting a light that made it seem as if small galaxies were orbiting around her head. Power radiated off her, silent and heavy, warping the kitchen. Blessing and Alex were staring just as hard as Bitter was, but the Assata kids were either averting their gazes or sneaking their admiring looks in, as if Sunflower wouldn't notice. Only Ube looked at her directly, as did Miss Bilphena.

Sunflower ignored both of them and walked up to Miss Virtue, who didn't move so much as a muscle on her face. They both looked out of place in the Assata kitchen, both with a sharpness to them that was perhaps just the edge of power making itself known. Everyone found themselves holding their breath. Sunflower's cheekbones were sculpted ridges cutting through her skin, and her eyes were dark as she searched Miss Virtue's face. The standoff held for a tense minute before Sunflower flashed a little smile, showing a gap between her front teeth that was also bridged with diamonds. "Interesting," she said in a low, husky rasp.

Miss Virtue tilted her head to one side. "Indeed."

They looked at each other for a few more moments before Sunflower gave a sharp nod and turned to leave the kitchen. "There has been no breach," she tossed over her shoulder.

Miss Bilphena stood up, clutching her robe around her, agitated. "Sunflower! She's clearly standing here."

"Yeah, thought you said no human being would ever make it through your wards," Ube added, but his voice was gentle, not confrontational.

Sunflower stopped at the door, and the look she threw to them was immensely amused. "Yes," she agreed. "Not a single human has ever made it through." And then she was gone, and only the faint hint of rose was left behind in the air. Everyone gaped in confusion, and Miss Virtue sighed.

"Can you address your security issues later?" she asked. "I need to know what the angels told you when they arrived.

Also, in case we've all forgotten, Lucille is slightly on fire. I think our new friends might have something to do with that."

Bitter raised a hand. "You think they set the fires?" she asked. Surely, Vengeance couldn't have been behind them. Bitter couldn't imagine the angel burning people alive, and yet . . . she was painfully aware that she didn't know what Vengeance was capable of, the lengths it would go to.

"We're not sure what's going on with those," Ube replied. "They got started last night, and the cops have been cracking down extra hard on the protesters for it. Several cop cars were set on fire, and we got word that a bunch of places are burning. The courthouse, the prison on the south side, all of the precincts."

Alex raised an eyebrow. "All eleven of them?"

"Apparently."

She grinned. "Sounds like a win to me."

Ube gave her a look. "We don't know what set it off. The protests have been continuing since last night, and the first wave of injuries is already larger than it's been in the past week combined."

"It's not Assata maintaining the protests? Or starting the fires?" Blessing asked.

Ube leaned forward in his chair. "You do realize that only some of us organize the protests, and we don't even gotta be out there for them to happen, right? The people of Lucille show up for themselves."

"It's a bold move to set the precincts on fire, though," Aloe said thoughtfully. "The cops are going to push back hard."

"It's the angels," Miss Virtue replied. "They're fond of fire as a symbol, a cleansing. With the new day comes a new world."

"How would you know?" Ube shot at her, his eyebrows drawn tightly together.

Miss Virtue bared her teeth in a polite smile that promised nothing and threatened quite a lot. "Fewer questions, more damage control. *What did they tell you?*"

Bitter exhaled and stepped forward to start the story from the beginning. She didn't look at Miss Virtue as she confessed how she'd called Vengeance out of the painting, how they'd seen the second angel in Alex's studio, then run into more in the atrium when they got to the safe house. "Hibiscus persuaded a bunch of the others to volunteer for the hunt, and then the angels vanished with them," she finished.

Miss Virtue was looking at her intently. "But you didn't volunteer? Even though you called out the first one?"

Bitter bristled. "I eh know it was going to be like this!"

"Yes, people rarely do when they pray." Miss Virtue tapped a marbled nail against the table. "So—they're hunting."

"It wasn't a prayer," Bitter objected.

The woman's gray eyes skimmed over her. "Wasn't it?" she retorted, but she didn't wait for Bitter's answer. "Based on what you told them or what the others might have told them, who do you think they will kill first?"

The casualness of her tone made Bitter feel sick. "I real hoping they won't kill anyone," she said.

Miss Virtue gave her a sympathetic look. "Come now, child."

"Vengeance said it would never hurt me!" Bitter's voice sounded futile even to her own ears.

"You are a gate. It *cannot* hurt you."

"Theron," said Blessing. "They'd go for Dian Theron first."

Miss Virtue raised an eyebrow. "A valid choice."

"Virtue!" Miss Bilphena glared at her. "You don't have to endorse the killing right in front of the kids."

"Look, if there's anyone who deserves to be hunted down by an angel, it's Theron," Miss Virtue said. "Am I still going to help stop that from happening? Sure. But let's not pretend he doesn't deserve some punishment."

One of the Assata kids dragged a whetstone along the blade of their machete. "He made a hundred billion dollars in a crisis, off the backs of his workers. They dropped like flies in the warehouses, or they went home and died like dogs. He deserves more than punishment." Someone else nudged them to be quiet, glancing worriedly at Ube, whose head was hanging down. The kitchen got uncomfortably silent before Ube lifted his head.

"No one knows better than I do the harm Theron has done," he said. "But we are not murderers, and his justice will not be death at Assata's hands."

"It's a bit late for that." Everyone whipped their heads around to see Eddie walking in slowly, her face even more swollen under the gauze. Several machetes clattered to the floor as Assata kids rushed to her side.

"Why are you up?" Aloe scolded. "I told you to stay in bed."

Eddie flapped a hand at him. "Then you shouldn't have let them update me last night. There's a fucking war going on." She sank gratefully into a chair that someone had pulled up for her and accepted a glass of water. Bitter wanted to say something, but her tongue felt too large and clumsy in her mouth. Eddie was surrounded by her friends, her people, in her home, and Bitter felt like an intruder, like she'd been shunted to the outside and had no right to be anywhere closer to her friend, who didn't even look her way. Her only consolation was how out of place Miss Virtue looked as well, even though she was as calm as if she owned the safe house. Just having the principal there made Bitter feel a little more anchored, like a piece of Eucalyptus was with her, like nothing could happen to her because the promises Miss Virtue made to her students extended through space and time, and it meant that Bitter would always be safe close to her.

"What do you mean, it's a bit late?" Ube asked as Aloe reached into his satchel and counted out some pain meds for Eddie.

She looked around the room with her good eye. "Has no one been monitoring our update channels?"

Alex glared at her. "We were a little preoccupied, what with the angels and then the breach." Bitter noticed how easily she'd slipped back into Assata, the unspoken affection that passed between her and Eddie.

"All the more reason," Eddie answered, shaking her head. "Everything's going to shit. They have Theron."

Ube's face went gray. "They *what*?"

"Yup. There's a contingent of angels and protesters moving him to the town square in plain fucking sight, taking on any cops who get in their way. Hibiscus and the others are with them, and they've blacked out everything. We're only active because Sunflower shields our channel."

Blessing moved closer to Alex and Bitter. "What the hell?" she whispered.

Alex wrapped her arms around her girlfriend and kissed her cheek. "Don't worry, baby. We're safe in here."

"Why are they moving him there?" Aloe asked.

Miss Virtue sighed and sat heavily in her chair. "Because

it's the center of Lucille. They're going to make an example out of him."

"What the fuck does that mean?"

"Show the monsters what's going to happen to them. Strike terror into their hearts." She looked up at them. "Have you ever seen what an angel does when it *wants* you to be afraid?"

For not the first time that morning, Bitter wondered how Miss Virtue knew the things she seemed to know. "Have you seen this happen before?" she asked the woman, her voice tentative.

Miss Virtue looked into a nowhere that was floating in the air. "A time too many," she replied. "History is so repetitive, you know."

The kids looked at each other. "What happens now?" Alex asked.

"If I were to make an educated guess," Miss Virtue said, "the first sacrifice is the bloodiest."

The color drained from Bitter's face. Her fears were growing legs and walking into reality. "They're going to kill him when they get to the town center."

"Yes, I believe you're right." Miss Virtue gave them all a somber look. "The angels will execute Theron in the heart of Lucille."

CHAPTER 13

The words swirled around in the kitchen, stunning everyone into silence. "They *wouldn't*," Blessing said. "They wouldn't just *execute* him."

Alex wasn't so sure. "You forgetting how pissed Hibiscus was? Together with the angels? Who's going to stop them?"

"*We* have to," Bitter said. Her blood felt cold, but the words still tripped their way out of her mouth. "I can't . . . I can't let Vengeance do this. I'm the one who called it out. If it kills someone, that's on me."

Aloe took her hand. "No, it's not, Bitter. Ignore whatever nonsense I said last night. You're not the one doing it, and it's not your fault."

"Doh talk like it already finish!" Bitter pulled away from him. He'd meant what he said in the hallway, and even if he'd been angry, it didn't mean he was wrong. Besides, this was so much bigger than Bitter's feelings or holding herself accountable. If Vengeance started bloodshed on such an enormous scale, with someone so powerful, what would the retaliation look like? How would the police react? Would the angels be able to get to all the monsters in time? Bitter remembered Eddie in Mr. Nelson's house, explaining that if there was no head to Assata, then it couldn't be cut off. The monsters in Lucille weren't like that. If you cut one of their heads off, how many more would spring up, hissing and desperate? Bitter couldn't look over at Eddie, who was acting like she didn't exist, speaking only to other Assata kids. Like Eddie had said, there was a war going on. It was ridiculous to think that those in power wouldn't fight with everything they had to keep the balance of Lucille skewed in their favor, angels or not. So that was that, Bitter decided. Theron dying was unthinkable. She had no idea what it would unleash, but she was certain that it would be nothing good. "I can't let this start."

"You can't go out there," Aloe countered.

Miss Bilphena raised her hand for silence. "He's right—you can't just go out there." She stood up and tightened her robe. "We will all go. Everyone, be ready to move out in fifteen."

Assata gave up a sharp cheer and raised their machetes, but Miss Bilphena shook her head. "No weapons. We will not raise up arms against our own."

Eddie folded her arms. "You sure Hibiscus is gonna feel the same way?"

A shadow of sadness passed over Miss Bilphena's face. "No," she answered. "I'm not sure at all. But I know *we* will not."

"What about the Elders who were supposed to come today?" Ube asked.

"I told them not to, after the breach." She glared at Miss Virtue. "Don't think I've forgotten about that, by the way."

"There will be plenty of time to harass me about getting through your precious wards," Miss Virtue said. "Let's just stop the angels from going on a murder spree for now." She seemed amused at how she'd turned the safe house upside down with her arrival, but she was the only one taking any pleasure from it. Several of the Assata kids still shot her mistrustful glares as they left the kitchen to go get ready. Miss Virtue caught Bitter's eye and winked at her.

Aloe tugged on Bitter's hand. "Come on," he said. "Let's get you something to eat."

Bitter followed him to where Alex and Blessing were pouring out bowls of cereal. Miss Bilphena came up to them, and a brief look of horror crossed her face.

"I know that's not what y'all tryna have for breakfast," she said. "Did you even eat last night?"

Bitter tried to think when last she had actually eaten.

"I'm not that hungry," she said, but it was half of a lie. Really, she just felt numb, like everything inside her that she recognized had been carved out and tossed aside, like she didn't know where to go and look for it, let alone find it again.

Aloe stared at her. "You didn't eat?"

"When did *you* eat?" she shot back.

"With Eddie! She had soup and I had pizza."

"Like Aloe would ever miss a meal," Blessing pointed out, and Alex snorted.

Miss Bilphena shook her head at them. "Thank goodness we made some real food this morning." She opened the door of a large toaster oven on the counter and started handing out bowls of cheesy grits that had been kept warm in there. "You have to eat, baby," she said to Bitter. "We don't go out on empty stomachs. You eat meat?" Bitter nodded and received a bowl with chunks of sausage and tomato sinking into the savory grits.

"Ooh, can I have one of those too?" Aloe asked. He and Bitter took their bowls to the table while Miss Bilphena handed Blessing a bowl with a fried egg and sliced avocado.

"You going to be okay going out there?" Aloe whispered to Bitter. "You don't have to go. We can handle it."

Bitter's stomach dropped. *Out there.* The protests were still happening, worse than ever with these fires, and Lucille was still the chaos she'd spent years hiding from. What had she been thinking when she'd said they had to stop the angels? To go right to the center of Lucille, where angels were holding the most powerful man in their society hostage? For a quick moment, Bitter was back at the Eucalyptus gate—what, just the day before?—panicking and running back inside. What would be different now? They were walking into a worse unknown, a scale of violence they literally could not begin to imagine, because who had ever heard of angels coming to shed blood for a revolution? But how would it look if she stayed back while everyone else went out there to stop the cascade she had started? She forced herself to take a deep breath. She was not the same girl who had frozen and run back the day before. She was someone who had painted an angel, brought it to life with her own blood, and faced it down. That had to count for something, the way her world had changed into an unrecognizable reality and she was still here, still breathing, still facing things. "I'll be okay," she told Aloe. "I'm not alone this time. You'll stay with me, right?"

Aloe kissed her shoulder, even though she couldn't feel it through her sweatshirt. "Of course," he said. "I'll stick with you the whole time."

- - - - -

Outside, Lucille looked both the same and completely different. There was so much smoke in the air that Miss Bilphena had made everyone put on masks before they left the safe house. Miss Virtue had refused. "Leave me and my lungs alone," she'd said, with a sharpness that brooked no disagreement. It wasn't difficult to confirm where the contingent holding Theron was heading. Crowds of Lucille citizens were flowing toward the city center, and the energy was almost crackling through the air, it was so tense.

"We just have to get to the angels," Ube said. He'd made Eddie stay behind, ordering her to rest, and had argued with Miss Bilphena until she agreed to stay as well and watch over the little children. Eddie still hadn't so much as looked at Bitter, and Bitter tried to pretend it didn't cut her as deeply as it did. Was Eddie mad at her? Did she blame her for the angels being here? There was no time for any of these questions, not with such a large crisis at hand.

"How the fuck are we gonna do that?" Alex asked. "You hear all those sirens? It's going to be chaos the closer we get."

"Leave that to me," Miss Virtue said, stepping to the front of their little group. "Don't walk past me and we should be fine." She narrowed her eyes at them and repeated the instruction. "Stay *behind* me, you hear?" A wall of stubborn silence greeted her question, and Miss Virtue raked a piercing gray look over all the Assata kids. "We not taking a damn step until y'all tell me you heard what I said." A round of grudging assents sounded off, and Miss Virtue nodded, her white snakeskin glistening in the sun. "Let's go."

It was unreal to witness. With every step she took, people moved out of her without even looking at her, not as if it was a conscious choice, but as if they suddenly had somewhere else to be, even if that was just a few yards away. Aloe kept Bitter in the center of their small group with Blessing and Alex, while the Assata kids took the perimeter.

"What did you tell them?" Bitter asked.

"The truth," Aloe replied. "You're not used to this and it could fuck you up."

Shame filled Bitter. They were going to think she was weak, she was a coward—everything she'd been trying so hard not to be. "I can handle it," she said, but her voice wobbled and tears stung her eyes. "You don't have to baby me."

Blessing and Alex both opened their mouths to object, but Ube spoke up before they did, pulling alongside Bitter. "Hey, listen," he said. "There is no shame in having anxiety around this. You don't have to force yourself through trauma just to prove something to us or yourself. We're trained to handle this. We just need to get you close to the angel, and we'll figure it out from there."

Bitter wiped tears from her eyes. "How? All I did was make a fucking mess by calling it through."

"Are you kidding me? You got some wild power in your art, Bitter. You saw how fucked up Lucille is, and you tried to make a difference. That's all we can do: try. We try over and over again, and sometimes it goes okay, sometimes it goes sideways. We'll find the angels and we'll try again. Okay?"

A muffled explosion sounded a few blocks away, and Bitter jumped, her hands trembling. Ube reached into his backpack and pulled out a pair of headphones. "Noise canceling," he said. "Put these on."

She knew he was telling her it was okay to not be okay, but Bitter couldn't hold back a sob, and suddenly she was crying, her feet stumbling over each other as she struggled to keep walking, the headphones useless in her hands. Ube let out a sharp, trilling whistle, and the group came to a halt. Miss Virtue looked back at them. "What's going on?"

"We need a moment," Ube said.

Bitter was trying her best to swallow her sobs, but they kept bubbling up, wet and loud and inconvenient. "I'm—I'm sorry," she choked out. "I'm so sorry." Aloe took the headphones from her hands as Blessing and Alex wrapped their arms around her.

"Babes. It's okay," they said. "We got you."

The Assata kids had formed a tight circle around the girls and Aloe. Ube was within the circle as well, with Miss Virtue standing next to him. She was watching the whole thing curiously. It looked like a protocol they had carried out many times before, standing shoulder to shoulder, some interlocking arms and others holding hands. They collectively took deep breaths, exhaling slowly and deliberately, their eyes closed and their heads bowed. Ube swiveled to drag his gaze over everyone, his face calm above his black mask. When he spoke, he kept his voice low, but it carried as clearly as if he was standing right behind each person, speaking into their ear.

"*We are each other's harvest,*" he said, and the others joined their voices to his, raising goose bumps along Bitter's arms. They sounded like they were remembering a prophecy, like they were making a world, reciting a prayer. "*We are each other's business. We are each other's magnitude and bond.*"

They repeated the lines two more times, then broke apart. Bitter's sobs had stilled into a tearful silence, and her friends were holding her hands. She couldn't muster up the words to thank the Assata kids, but they gave her small smiles and nods and everyone started walking again.

"Gwendolyn Brooks," Miss Virtue said to Ube as they moved forward. "You still speak those lines. She has been dead for many decades."

"Her words will never die," he replied. "They remind us that we are all in service to one another, we are not separate." A wistfulness entered his eyes. "Hibiscus has a hard time remembering that. So do a lot of the others."

"Pain does that to people." Miss Virtue looked up at the clouded sky. "You all are so young to be doing this work."

Ube shrugged. "Someone has to. The older folk mean well, but they still got ideas about respectability and working through the system. That shit ain't gonna save none of us. The angel had a point when it said the world gotta burn before we can build a new one. We just got different ideas about what kinda fire we need, you know?"

Miss Virtue looked amused. "How do you know your way is the right way?"

"I don't. But we moving with love, and I figure that can't be wrong."

She raised an eyebrow. "Even for the monsters?"

Ube had dark shadows under his eyes. "If you're asking me if I hate them, the answer is no. My mama didn't raise me like that. I want to stop Theron more than the others do, shit. I just don't think killing him is the way to go."

"A different type of fire."

"Exactly."

They were close to the city center now. Bitter could see Eucalyptus's buildings standing up against the sky. For a second, she thought about just breaking out of the pack and running, running until she was through that side gate and up the stairs and back in her room as if none of this had happened, except there was a charred panel of wood there that would remind her that her world had changed, her paintings were no longer safe, and she could no longer hide. The group stopped walking, and Miss Virtue cocked her head to listen to the commotion.

"They're already at the center," she said. "We're running out of time."

"We're like a block away," Aloe said. "What do we do?"

Ube glanced around. "Aight, Assata, to me. Eucalyptus, y'all post up in that alley for a few minutes, okay? We're going to get closer and see what the situation looks like. We'll be right back."

"Five minutes," Miss Virtue said, then melted away into a gaggle of people.

"Where the fuck is she going?" Alex asked.

"No fucking idea. Doesn't matter." Ube turned to leave. "And I mean it, stay there. We don't have time to be looking for people." He went off with the Assata kids while Bitter drew back into the alley with her friends. It was a dead end, which made her feel better, like no one could sneak up behind them.

Blessing poked Alex. "How come you didn't go with Ube?"

Alex leaned over and gave her a quick kiss. "I'm Eucalyptus now, I told you. I'm right where I'm supposed to be."

"Why did you leave Assata?" The question spilled out of Bitter unintentionally, and she clapped her hands over her mouth. "Oh shit. I eh mean to say that out loud."

Alex chuckled. "It's cool. I just got burned out. Wanted to make things."

"They didn't mind?"

"Eh, some of them did. The ones who mattered didn't."

"Did you ever feel . . . guilty?"

"For not being in the trenches anymore? Fuck no. That shit is brutal." She bent over and wiped some dust off her boots, then straightened back up. "Like, I got mad respect for my Assata folk, for sure. But we all know what it takes out of you, so yeah, most people get it when you have to tap out. Some folk just chill at the house, you know, work with the babies, work in the garden. There's always a ton of admin work for all our programs—the free breakfasts, the rent assistance, all of it. I wanted to learn shit you can only get at Eucalyptus. I think they woulda been more chill about it if I'd tapped out but still stayed."

"Wow. I used to think allyuh had to be, like, doing front-line shit."

Alex laughed. "Nah, that's wild. Don't trust any movement

that's tryna make martyrs out of kids, man. We not even twenty-one yet."

Bitter turned her head to look down the alley, losing focus on the conversation for a minute. She thought she'd heard something rustle back there. Aloe and Alex were talking about back when the drinking age used to be twenty-one. "Wild, right?" he was saying. "But then they'd give you a gun soon as you turn eighteen."

"Old enough to die, not old enough to drink."

The sound came again, and Bitter took a step back. "Allyuh hearing that?" she asked. She wasn't about to head toward it alone, not in a dim and dead-end alley on a day like today. The rest of them fell silent, and then the sound came again, this time weaker.

Blessing stepped back as well. "See now, I think this is where we dip the fuck out immediately."

"Ube said not to leave, though," Bitter replied.

"You wanna get jumped in an alley, be my fucking guest. I vote for leaving right now."

"Hold up," Alex said, taking slow steps forward.

"That is a nonmelanated decision if I've ever seen one," Blessing muttered. "Why she moving *toward* the creepy sound?"

"Nah, I think there's someone back there," Alex continued, squinting.

"That's not helping your case, my love." Her girlfriend was starting to look really worried. "Please come back?"

"Lemme go with her," Aloe said. "You two stay ready, okay?"

"Been ready." Blessing looked like she was about to burst into a sprint any second.

Alex took another step, then gestured to Aloe, who came up to her. They both leaned forward; then Alex pulled a small flashlight from her jacket pocket and shone the light down the alley. Her face went stricken. "Mr. Nelson!" She dashed forward, and Aloe cast a confused glance back at the girls before following her.

Bitter and Blessing looked at each other, Bitter's heart grinding to a painful stop in her chest. She had to have heard wrong.

"The watermelon man?" Blessing asked. "Can't be."

They came up to the others, and Bitter felt like screaming because Alex had been right. It was Mr. Nelson lying on the ground, his head cradled on Alex's thighs. His salt-and-pepper hair was coiled tight to his scalp, and his beard clung to his cheeks and jaw. He was wearing blue-and-white-striped overalls and one boot, and his other foot was covered in a white sock that seemed stained with blood. When Bitter looked closer, she could see that his overalls were darkened around his midsection too. His eyes were closed. Alex put her fingers to his neck.

"I can barely get a pulse. Fuck!"

Aloe was kneeling next to her, moving his hands gently over Mr. Nelson's body. "He's still alive. We need to get him to a hospital right now."

He'd fed Bitter pie. He'd invited her into his home and fed her pie, and now he was lying alone in a dead-end alley. Her hands began to shake. There wasn't a Lucille without Mr. Nelson. He was there with his truck parked in front of the library every summer, posted up on a folding chair with a book while a wealth of watermelons stood stacked next to him. Just like in his house, a few minutes with him could turn Lucille into a place that was hopeful and beautiful, where you could almost forget what it was turning into.

"Should we move him, though?" Blessing asked. "He looks badly hurt."

Aloe grimaced. "He's not going to make it out here. You still got a pulse, Alex?"

Alex's face was drawn tight. "Barely."

The panic was loud in Bitter, throwing itself against her ribs. There was no reason Mr. Nelson should be out here, injured and alone in an empty alley, unless it had something to do with the ongoing chaos. He couldn't die. He had to be okay. Ethel was waiting for him, hopefully safe in their house. Bitter could remember how soft his voice was whenever he mentioned his wife. He *had* to go home to her. There was no other option. "Maybe Vengeance can heal him," she found herself saying, and everyone looked at her, confused. "It healed my arm back at Eucalyptus, when I called it out."

"Your angel's out there with Theron and the others," Blessing pointed out.

"I know, but—" There was that ache in her stomach, the tug she'd felt back at the Assata house when she was near Vengeance. "I think we're connected. I think maybe I could call it?"

"You better hurry up, then," Alex said curtly. "He's fading fast."

Bitter nodded and closed her eyes, focusing on the slightly sick feeling in her belly, like something was off balance. She pulled up an image of Vengeance in her mind, scaled head and yellow eyes, egg-white spine and long claws, its whole length of smoke. The ache in her stomach intensified, and for a second Bitter could almost *feel* Vengeance's awareness of her, even from blocks away. "Please come," she whispered. "I need your help."

A sharp pain shot through her, and Bitter groaned, doubling over. Aloe rushed to her side. "B, you okay? What happened?"

The air in the alley shook as a guttural voice ripped

through it. "She called me," Vengeance said. All of them gasped and jumped back. The angel was a few feet away, its seven yellow eyes narrowed as it looked at them. "You interrupt the hunt, child."

"Is it still a hunt if you already caught Theron?" Blessing asked, then flinched as Vengeance looked at her. Aloe was breathing in short, sharp gasps, and Bitter remembered that this was his first time seeing the angel. She reached for his hand, but Aloe was backing away from Vengeance, stumbling until he was pressed against the alley wall.

"It is still a hunt until the prey is dead," Vengeance was saying.

Bitter stepped forward. "I need you to heal a friend of ours," she said, pointing to Mr. Nelson. His head was still resting on Alex, his eyes still closed, his mouth slightly open. "We don't know how he got hurt."

Vengeance looked around the alley, its gaze sweeping the street outside. "There have been . . . skirmishes," it said. "There has been some collateral damage. Your police only understand brute force. It is regrettable."

"You're not even looking at him!" Bitter was starting to get upset. "Can you just heal him, please?"

Vengeance glanced down at Mr. Nelson. "That human is dead," it said. "I cannot heal him."

Bitter stared at it. "What?"

Alex pressed her fingers to Mr. Nelson's neck, then inhaled a sharp breath. "It's gone," she said, her voice trembling. "His pulse is gone." Aloe burst into motion, moving in to give CPR, his hands pressing on Mr. Nelson's chest, his mouth blowing breath into his lungs.

"His spirit is not coming back." Vengeance watched them, tilting its head slowly to one side. "Why do you continue?"

"Because we're not fucking monsters," Blessing yelled, tears filling her eyes.

"Heal him," Bitter insisted, refusing to look over at the old man or Aloe's desperate attempts. Mr. Nelson could not die. Her voice rose in a hiss. "*I know you can heal him*. He was alive just a moment ago!"

"Now he is not." Vengeance looked down at her. "This is the way of mortality, little gate. He has crossed over."

Bitter felt a loud madness seeping into her head. "Then bring him back!" she screamed at the angel. He had fed her pie. Eddie loved him. "*Bring him back!*"

Vengeance stretched its dark mouth. "Angels cannot resurrect." It raised its head and looked off into the distance. "Worlds burn when we return. There is always blood."

Rage was blurring Bitter's vision, thickening her veins, cutting the bottom of her tongue. "He was innocent! You're supposed to *protect* the innocent!"

The angel glanced back at her. "Blood is blood," it said.

"There are no new worlds without sacrifice." Then, as suddenly as it had appeared, Vengeance vanished, and the four of them were left in the alley, alone with the body of a man who had done nothing but bring sweetness into their lives.

CHAPTER 14

Aloe had to drag Bitter out of the alley. Her rage was incandescent, rolling off her in furious, grieving waves.

"We cyah leave him there!" she yelled. How on earth would she explain that to Eddie? How would any of them explain it to Mrs. Nelson, his Ethel? That they'd left him alone and cold in a deserted alley, like no one loved him. Alex had taken off her jacket and draped it over his face, a leafy green shroud, but it wasn't enough. None of it was enough. Mr. Nelson deserved so much more.

"We'll come back for him," Aloe promised. "You think any of us want to leave him here like this?"

Bitter didn't care. "I hate Vengeance," she spat out. "I hate it, I hate it, *I hate it*! How could it say all of that? It could have saved him!"

Blessing's eyes were red from crying as she put her arm around Bitter. "I don't think it thinks like us," she said.

"It does think like a fucking monster." Bitter hissed the

words as she stood with her friends at the mouth of the alley. "It can go to hell."

The others exchanged worried looks just as one of the Assata kids returned, pulling down his mask to update them. "Everyone's gathered in the park," he said. "Let's go."

Blessing and Aloe flanked Bitter, propelling her along, because every fiber in her was calling her back to the dead-end alley. She wanted to stay there with Mr. Nelson and be done with this. It was obscene that the rest of the world could move on, that they could continue with a mission as if his life stopping wasn't the atrocity that it was. Blessing seemed shaken, but Aloe and Alex were eerily calm. Bitter wondered if that was what it meant to work with Assata, if death started to mean something else.

"We shouldn't have left him," she whispered to Blessing.

Her best friend glanced at her and seemed to pick up on her feelings in a heartbeat. "Hey, we're doing the right thing," Blessing whispered back. "There will be more like him if we don't stop the angels, remember?" She squeezed Bitter's arm as they reached the outskirts of the central park. The energy there was at a fever pitch, and the park was full of people, pressed so close together that no one could see the city square in the middle of it. Lucille had seen the angels, and its citizens were frantic with a mixture of fear and hope and bloodthirsty excitement. They were chanting together, words thudding into the air, weighted with anger and years upon years of injustice. "Eat the rich! Eat the rich!"

The Assata kid who had come to get them looked worried. "It's escalated," he said. "I was only gone for a few minutes—what the fuck?"

Ube came up to them. "The angel is . . . convincing." Miss Virtue was behind him with the rest of the crew. He looked at Bitter, who was standing with her fists and jaw clenched tight. "You ready to go in?" he asked her. She nodded grimly, holding on to Blessing's words. There couldn't be more deaths, more Mr. Nelsons. She wouldn't allow it.

"All right," Miss Virtue said. "Behind me."

They gathered quickly, and she started moving toward the center of the crowd. "How come I cyah see Vengeance?" Bitter asked. "Even with all these people, we should be able to see the angels."

"Unless they went back to those smaller shapes," Alex said. "You know, to not scare the humans."

Miss Virtue snorted lightly. "Wise of them," she said, and there was something sour in the back of her voice. Bitter glanced over at her but then stumbled as she was shoved by the crowd. There were too many people in the park, bodies amassed thickly, and those who were trying to get out of Miss Virtue's way had nowhere to go.

Dread began to crawl down Bitter's spine, but she shoved

209

it away, replacing it with anger. "We're not going to get there in time," she said.

"We will try," Miss Virtue replied, pushing through, her white suit a snakeskin beacon homing in on the angels. The chanting suddenly stopped, and an uncanny hush spread over the park before Vengeance's voice glitched through, ice cold and charming. Psychopathic, now that Bitter thought about it. The voice of a thing that understood nothing about life.

"It is time for a purge," it said, and the trees shook from the volume of its voice. "Evil has lived in Lucille for too long, and it must be cleansed."

Miss Virtue was still trying to get through the crowd, and it seemed like they were a little closer now. "Almost there," she said over her shoulder. Bitter could see the angels now, and yes, Vengeance was back in its vaguely human form, standing with the other angels in a semicircle behind it. Theron was there, his hands bound behind his back, his mouth gagged. His skin was pale and clammy, and his eyes were wide with naked terror, but he seemed unharmed. He looked nothing like he did in the headlines and on the news, where he was always polished, always gleaming with the fat of billionaire wealth. Every photograph Bitter had ever seen of him had Theron wearing a small smirk, like nothing and no one could ever touch him. Except, today, something terrible had.

"Is this man a monster?" Vengeance asked the crowd, and they roared assent with a thousand throats. Vengeance looked at Theron with its unforgiving yellow eyes, and Theron whimpered, cowering away from the angel. He didn't look like a monster to Bitter then, even though she knew what he was, what he'd done. He just looked like a weak man, his expensive pants wet where he'd pissed himself, humiliated in front of the whole of Lucille. Bitter didn't know how she felt about seeing him like that, but she couldn't summon the wild brightness she saw in the eyes of so many in the crowd. It looked like something contagious, something that bared their teeth and pulled at their skin. Was this what justice looked like? This frantic hunger?

Vengeance stretched its mouth into a smile, and Bitter's blood crackled around the edges. "All monsters must die," it said.

Miss Virtue stopped short with a gasp, whirling around just as Vengeance grasped Theron's head. Bitter's vision was suddenly enveloped in the cool white of Miss Virtue's suit as the woman pressed her close, blocking her view. "Don't look, baby girl."

Bitter opened her mouth to say something, but the sound of a sharp crack took over, piercing through her ears and stabbing into her head. It was followed by a dull thud of something heavy being dropped, and Bitter knew with a clear and sick certainty that Vengeance had snapped Theron's neck like it was nothing, like a human life was *nothing* to it. Blessing gave a short, strangled scream, but Bitter couldn't break free of the principal's hold to turn to her best friend. Her whole world was the echo of those short death sounds and the white blur of Miss Virtue pressed against her face. To her surprise, the crowd did not cheer. There was a horrified silence; then Bitter heard someone gag and a child begin to cry. She wondered who would have brought a child out to something like this, her mind skirting the horror of what had just happened, pushing her into numbness. Miss Virtue released her, and light stung Bitter's eyes.

It was strange to be so close to the principal, to have been wrapped in her arms. Bitter was sure Miss Virtue had hugged her at some point in the years she'd been at Eucalyptus, but her memory felt fuzzy. Everything felt blurred, like she couldn't be sure who or what was real. Miss Virtue's presence was still an anchor—nothing bad could happen to Bitter when she was with the woman, although now she was learning that Miss Virtue couldn't stop other terrible things from happening. Bitter wanted to reach out a hand to Blessing, who was sobbing quietly, but her muscles felt frozen and stiff. Theron was dead. Theron was *dead*?

"We have to go," Miss Virtue was saying. "Quickly now."

Vengeance was speaking again, but its voice was a loud ringing in her ears above the maddened rush of blood in her veins. Miss Virtue was leading all of them out of the park at a much faster pace than they'd entered it. People got out of their way without thinking, moving in shock now that they were no longer pressing to see the front. It was a surprise that they weren't stampeding, but Bitter didn't think she would've moved either if Miss Virtue hadn't commanded them to. There was something about the angels that had fixed her feet to the ground once Theron's neck had snapped, like the world had become immediately different, something you couldn't flee from, like staying motionless meant perhaps it would pass you over. Where was there to go? The very air of Lucille had changed, and it smelled like a different kind of death.

Aloe grabbed Bitter's hand and she looked up at him, but his face was indistinct. She realized that her eyes were veiled with tears. Theron was dead. Vengeance had executed the most powerful man in Lucille and dropped his body in front of everyone like he was a bag of trash, just being thrown out, just being cleared. There was blood, and she didn't know how much of it was on her hands, because *she* had started this, *she* had called the angel through with her terrible wants. She had wanted to be a monster, to summon something monstrous to get rid of Lucille's monsters, and now Bitter didn't know who was the monster or where the lines that described it started or stopped. Did those lines reach into her? Was Vengeance still carrying out her wants or its own? Had she wanted Theron to become inanimate flesh, sudden meat slapping against the floor? Blessing had seemed to agree with the angels that monsters needed to die, and yet here she was, sobbing while Alex held her. Bitter stared at them through her tears. Alex was dry-eyed, but her skin was drawn. Maybe none of them knew what they wanted.

Miss Virtue led them to the edge of the park and was about to turn down a street when Ube stopped her. "There's Hibiscus," he said.

Bitter turned to look, and sure enough, there was Hibiscus with the other Assata kids who had chosen to go with the angels. They were under an awning, separate from the crowd, and as one of them moved aside, Bitter saw who they were gathered around.

"They have the mayor," she said, shocked. His hands were bound like Theron's were, and he was bleeding from a gash on his head.

"Oh fuck," Alex said, and the skin around her mouth went bloodless with tension. "Is he next?"

Blessing looked like she was about to throw up. Bitter

broke away from them and ran over to Hibiscus. She shoved him in the chest, not caring that he was so much bigger than her. "Yuh happy now?" she yelled. "It feeling like justice to you yet?"

Miss Virtue and the others joined her. Hibiscus looked pale. "I—I didn't know . . ."

Alex drew her fist back, then shook out her hand. "I really wanna punch out your goddamn stupid face," she said. "What d'you *mean*, you didn't know? They told you from jump they were gonna kill him!"

Hibiscus shook his head, his voice tangled with confusion, an uncertain wildness flickering in his eyes. "I didn't know it would feel like this," he said. "Like, we've seen people die before, but this? This shit ain't the same. It doesn't . . . it don't feel right."

"Glad to see you're catching up," Ube said flatly. He looked over at the others who were with Hibiscus. "How about y'all? You still fiending to see more people die?"

They glanced at each other and shook their heads. "Nah, those things are scary as fuck," the girl in red said, looking shaken. "They don't—they don't *care* about anything."

"So maybe let the mayor go," Blessing suggested. "We don't have to keep this shit going."

Hibiscus stepped in front of the man. "We can't do that,"

he said. "He's been loyal to Theron for years. The council listens to him. We can't just let him go."

"You cyah let the angels kill him either," Bitter snapped. "You realize they never going to stop, right? It go just be executions and executions, over and over again, for anyone they decide is a monster."

Miss Virtue glanced back at the crowd. Its energy was finally shifting, horror and shock morphing into terror and the seeds of panic. "We have to leave right now," she said. "Things are about to scatter, and I promised Miss Bilphena I would get all her kids back to the safe house before it got ugly."

Ube turned to Hibiscus and the rest of the splintered Assata faction. "Y'all ready to come back?" he asked. "We can figure this out at home."

Hibiscus hesitated, then nodded. "Okay," he said. "We didn't lead them to the rest of the council yet—it was just Theron and the mayor."

The boy with long braids looked sick to his stomach. "They killed Theron's entire security detail," he said. "As if it was nothing."

Miss Virtue looked grim. "Sounds about right. Come on. We'll take the mayor back with us." Sunlight reflected off her suit as she turned sharply and began to lead them through Lucille, away from the murderous angels and back to the wards of the Assata house.

Miss Bilphena sent the little children upstairs when the crew returned, shaking her head at the sight of the mayor, who they had blindfolded. "Really?" she said. "We taking political prisoners now?"

"They killed Theron," Ube replied, his voice dull. "Snapped his neck in front of the whole of Lucille."

"What?" Miss Bilphena closed the door behind them.

"Yup." Ube turned to Hibiscus. "Take him to the atrium?" Hibiscus nodded, seemingly relieved to have Ube making the calls again, and led the mayor away. Miss Virtue sighed and shrugged off her jacket. She was wearing a white button-down shirt underneath with a snakeskin vest.

"Tea?" Miss Bilphena offered.

"Yes, please." Miss Virtue walked with her into the kitchen and sat down, unbuttoning her cuffs and rolling her sleeves up. "Chamomile, if you have it." The gas stove clicked as a ring of blue fire erupted under the kettle, and Bitter leaned against the kitchen wall, letting her legs give way until she was sitting on the floor. Blessing sat down next to her.

"How you feeling, babe? This shit is wild."

Bitter reached out and squeezed her best friend's hand. "I real sorry I dragged you into this," she said. Blessing's eyes looked haunted by what she had seen in the park. She adjusted her hijab around her face and summoned up a little smile.

"It's not your fault," she said. "All of this just got outta control." Alex and Aloe joined them, passing out bags of potato chips.

Bitter refused hers. "I not hungry."

Aloe pressed it into her hand anyway. "Doesn't matter. You still have to eat."

"I can't believe it killed him," Alex said, sitting cross-legged on the tile. "It looked like it was snapping a toothpick or some shit." Blessing smacked her arm. "Ow! What?"

Bitter felt sick. "I should've done more to stop it."

"You did everything you could," Aloe said. "We can't change what's happened—we just have to somehow figure out how to stop it from killing the mayor."

Blessing's eyes went wide. "How long do you think before it comes here looking for him?" They all stared at each other.

"Shit," Alex said, and put down the rest of her chips. "She's right. It's gonna come right back here, and it's gonna be pissed."

Bitter pushed herself up from the floor. "That's fine," she said, remembering Mr. Nelson's face breaking open into a smile as he watched her taste the sweet potato pie in his kitchen just yesterday. Now he was lying gray and cold out in that alley with Alex's jacket over him, all because of the angel. "I real pissed too."

Miss Virtue took her cup of tea from Miss Bilphena with a grateful smile. "Shall we join the others in the atrium?"

When they got there, the mayor was standing with his blindfold off, his eyes flicking from side to side in alarm. His hair was tousled and his clothes were rumpled, but he had his spine straight, like he was trying to be ready, to not collapse under the weight of the day. Hibiscus and the rest of Assata were milling about, keeping an eye on him but also talking amongst themselves in low agitated whispers.

Bitter felt the tug in her stomach intensify suddenly. She winced, and Aloe took her arm. "What's wrong?" he asked.

"I think Vengeance is close," she said. Her words had Assata exploding into action; no one even paused to question her. They formed a blockade around the mayor, not bothering with weapons because they already knew they would be useless against the angels. Hibiscus's eyes searched the air, looking to see where the angel would come from. Ube's jaw was tight, and Aloe grabbed hold of Bitter's hand, giving her a firm look of solidarity. Blessing and Alex were standing shoulder to shoulder, and the air in the atrium was tight with fearful anticipation.

Vengeance materialized in the same spot it had disappeared from the last time, right under the weeping willow.

It was back in its full form, all smoke and seven angry eyes with a bloodstained mouth. The willow branches drifted right through it like it was a ghost. Bitter felt the tug in her stomach twist and then dissipate. She was taking a deep breath to step forward and confront this creature she'd made, who had her blood on its mouth and Theron's on its hands, but Miss Virtue gently stopped her with a hand on her shoulder. Bitter looked up at her.

"What are you doing?" she asked. "I have to handle Vengeance."

Miss Virtue didn't even look at her. "Not this time," she replied, and there was something eerie about her voice. It was layered now, like the words were slipping and rasping against each other. Vengeance swiveled its scaled head in Miss Virtue's direction, the eggshells along its spine clacking together in rattling succession. As soon as it saw her, the yellow of its eyes flared and it swelled in size, nearly doubling. Bitter gasped and stepped back as the Assata kids scrambled out of the way of the mutating smoke slamming through the air of the atrium. Miss Virtue didn't even blink. Vengeance let out a low growl, filled with more malevolence than Bitter had ever heard from the angel since she'd called it out of the painting.

"Traitor," it hissed, and its voice was a thousand knives

scraping over taut glass, forcing everyone in the atrium to clap their hands over their ears, collectively wincing as the sound bled into their skulls.

Miss Virtue gave it an empty smile. "It's good to see you again, sib."

CHAPTER 15

Bitter's jaw dropped as she whipped her head between Miss Virtue and Vengeance. They *knew* each other?

"Do not call me *sibling*," Vengeance snarled. "You have lost that privilege."

The principal shrugged. "What we call a thing does not change what it is."

"I'm sorry," Bitter interrupted. "Miss Virtue? What's happening?"

"Virtue?" The angel reared its scaly head in contempt, bringing its size back down. "That is the name you chose?"

"You call yourself Vengeance," Miss Virtue replied. "It's hardly subtle."

"I am here *hunting*. Your only task was to watch the gates, and you have failed woefully at that."

Nothing about their conversation was making any sense to Bitter. She looked up at Miss Virtue. "Watch the gates?" she asked. "What's it talking about?"

Miss Virtue didn't take her eyes off Vengeance. "I *was* watching the gates. *You* changed the timelines, veiled things from me."

Vengeance growled and its smoke rippled. "Because we knew your allegiance had shifted!"

"Wait," Bitter interrupted again. "Aren't *we* the gates?"

Vengeance glanced at her. "Yes, child. The gates have always been gates. It was important to collect them in one place, for when the time would come."

Aloe edged closer to Bitter. "What are they talking about?" he asked.

Bitter barely heard him. She was staring at Miss Virtue, flashes of memory burning across her mind. The social worker. The pattern of rescue. Eucalyptus. It all coalesced into a sharp picture that cut across her heart. "You were *collecting* us?" Everything Vengeance had been saying to Miss Virtue was falling into place, making a terrible sense. "You . . . you knew this would happen? That they would come through our work?"

Miss Virtue sighed impatiently. Her shirt was slightly wrinkled, but she still managed to look immaculate, a sliver too perfect. "It was hardly a hobby, Bitter."

Bitter was still struggling to reconcile the implications, the long arm they had, the way they reached into her life, her own past. "But that would mean you been working with the angels this whole time?"

Time seemed impossible to process in that moment. How long had Eucalyptus been open? Had that been its function all along? If this was true, then Miss Virtue had been giving them a safe place not because she cared, not because she was protecting them, but because they were going to be *useful*. As if they were tools, not people. And from the way Vengeance spoke about people, Bitter already knew that to be true. It had all been a lie, every brick in every wall of the school had been a lie from the beginning.

Bitter took a gasping step away from Miss Virtue, betrayal flowering in her chest like a wildfire. She felt Aloe grab her hand, his palm cool and textured against hers, a new anchor as she spun adrift. "How could you?" she asked, her voice splintering. "You told us we were *safe*."

The rest of the Eucalyptus kids were staring at Miss Virtue with mirrored expressions of hurt and shock glassed into their eyes. Alex was clenching her hands so tightly that her knuckles jutted out against her skin, and Blessing had wrapped her arms around herself, her mouth trembling. Miss Virtue had collected all of them, gathered them together under the roof of a lie, and made them love her. Aloe wiped a furious tear off his face, and the Assata kids looked on, unconsciously huddling closer to Miss Bilphena. Sunflower had joined them, small glittered lights twinkling off her black agbada.

A few feet away, the mayor was standing with his back pressed to the wall, frozen, his eyes dilated in terror. He was still keeping his spine straight, his shoulders back, but he looked like a toy, a doll propped up to the side for the time being. Blood washed down one side of his face in a faint drying river from the cut on his head.

"I used to work with them," Miss Virtue admitted slowly, taking in the faces of her students as if it had just occurred to her that they would be upset at the news. "And then I stopped."

Vengeance made a rotten and rattling sound in the back of its throat. "*Traitor,*" it spat. "You lie to the child even in the truths you tell."

"Why did you stop?" Grief was coarse in Bitter's throat, but she was still hoping that there was a fragment in there she could salvage, something she could understand. If she could just *understand,* maybe she wouldn't lose Eucalyptus. Maybe this whole life wouldn't turn out to be a lie, like every other home before it.

Miss Virtue's eyes softened, the gray going from a battling steel to a soft rain cloud. "I met all of you," she said, emotion thickening her voice. "And you were not *gates,* you were entire little worlds. You were more important than the use they had planned for you. They don't understand humans, they never have. I thought—" She shook her head and bit her lip, slicing a sharp look in Vengeance's direction. "I thought

I had more time before they would come. They gave me no warning."

"You thought you could keep us out," Vengeance snarled. "You fool. We are inevitable."

Miss Virtue bared her teeth at the angel, and Bitter got that sense again that they were sharper than they should be. "You are apocalyptic," the principal growled. "I have no desire to see you reduce their world to ruin, as you do so well."

Vengeance snaked its head to one side and blinked at her slowly, each of its yellow eyes scaling down, then back up. "The world always ends," it said. "It is of no consequence. Never place your loyalty with flesh." The angel was beginning to sound like it was running out of patience. There was a horrifying indifference coating all its words, and Bitter realized that it had none of the righteousness it had first spoken to her with when it had scorched its way out of the painting. It didn't sound like it was on a crusade of justice anymore—it sounded like it was there for a cleanup job and they were getting in its way. "You don't care about us," Bitter said slowly. "You were only protecting me because I's useful to you. You don't care about humans in general."

"*Humans* don't care about humans in general," Vengeance spat, animosity dripping from its voice. "We are restoring what your people already contaminated. It is a cycle, it is a ritual, and yes, it is bloody. But a new world springs up in the clots of it."

"You have killed enough," Miss Virtue said, her voice darkening. "Innocent people have died for your hunt."

"What are a few lives for the greater good?" Vengeance replied, its yellow eyes unmoving. "We executed a monster." It glanced toward the mayor. "We will execute another. And another, until Lucille is cleansed, until the purge is complete."

"You want to drown the streets in endless blood." Miss Virtue curled her lip. "You call that justice?"

"*Yes,*" the angel hissed. "You have watched the humans for decades! Their world is corrupt. What else but blood can wash it clean?" Its smoke pulsed and rippled, bulging out from its body. "You interrupt the hunt, traitor. Leave us now." Bitter watched in horror as Vengeance turned to the mayor, whose spine finally gave out as he crumpled to the floor, saliva dribbling from his mouth, fear rendering him incoherent. Miss Virtue stepped in front of the man. Even with all her height, she looked tiny compared to Vengeance, who towered above her in unnatural feet of compressed smoke and paint and blood.

"Step aside," Vengeance commanded.

Miss Virtue didn't move. "No. This hunt needs to *end,*

angel. Return to where you came from, and take the others with you."

Vengeance's scaled face sharpened with hostile intent. A cold foreboding filled Bitter's heart. "It going to kill her," she whispered, almost to herself.

Aloe's hand was sweating in hers, damp and firm. "It wouldn't," he replied, but there was no certainty in his voice.

"You doh understand," Bitter said, her voice thin. "It won't let anything stand in its way." She was beginning to understand how single-minded Vengeance was, how little it mattered what any of them said to it, why it had been unmoved when she'd begged for Mr. Nelson's life in the alley. The angel simply did not *care*. It could not be convinced or debated with.

"Step aside, traitor," Vengeance said coldly. "Or you will be gutted like the humans you betrayed us for." The angel had been translucent this whole time, willow branches sweeping through its form, but now it raised its claws and they became solid, more solid than reality, the air around them warping with their new weight. All sound evaporated from Bitter's throat. She thought she was screaming for it to stop, but her mouth was empty, stretched open and futile. Miss Virtue didn't move. Vengeance swiped down, so fast that Bitter didn't see its arm move. One moment it was raising its claws, and the next they were embedded in Miss Virtue's stomach, hooked right below her rib cage. The atrium fell silent as a howl choked and died inside Bitter.

Miss Virtue should have screamed. She should have *screamed,* skewered on the end of an angel's arm. Her voice should have filled the air with agony, but instead her head jerked back, the tendons in her neck stretched and thick, then snapped forward, and Bitter heard bones crack. Miss Virtue was smiling wider than should have been possible for a human.

"Many thanks, sib," she said to Vengeance, and her voice was an unfamiliar metallic thing, iron grating over stone. "I have been starved for so long." Her suit went up in ghostly white flames that lit up the atrium, and as her clothes burned into nothing, her flesh turned gray, her skin calcifying into stone, her hair and eyes hardening into rock. Vengeance roared and ripped its limb from her torso. There was a wet and sickening sound as its claws broke off in Miss Virtue, leaving seeping wounds on the angel's limb that leaked white smoke. Vengeance stumbled back, its yellow eyes flickering wildly.

"*Impossible,*" it said. "You were stripped." The smoke cauterized its wounds, leaving a stump where its claws used to be.

Miss Virtue's body was flaring out, expanding into an

unfamiliar shape, stone groaning as her bones gave way to something else, something very loudly not of this world. "It was a terrible fall," she concurred, her deadened eyes fixed on Vengeance. "No other angels to sacrifice a piece of themselves so I might regain a memory of what I used to be."

Behind her, the mayor's eyes rolled into white as he went into a dead faint.

Bitter and Aloe backed up until they bumped into Sunflower. Aloe's hand was clenched tightly around Bitter's.

"What the fuck?" he choked out. "What *is* she?"

"Like I said," Sunflower said through tight teeth, her arms folded. *"That's not a human."*

Miss Virtue was now as tall as Vengeance, standing several feet above the rest of them. With a grinding rumble, wings started to extend from her back, four on each side, snapping open in a cloud of silvery dust. Bitter flinched when she saw that each wing was tipped with more of Miss Virtue's eyes, that searing gray she had come to know so well. Her jaw went slack with awe. "You're an *angel*," she gasped, shock gathering under her tongue.

Miss Virtue glanced down at her and, much to Bitter's surprise, winked. "Do not be afraid," she said, the words clanging into the air.

For the first time since Bitter had called it out of the painting, Vengeance looked unsure. It took a few steps back, its smoke bubbling uncomfortably. A flake of Bitter's dried blood detached from the corner of its mouth and floated down to the grass. She watched it fall, a low ringing sound building in her ears.

Had it been barely a day ago that she'd cut her arm open and fed the angel out of the painting? How strange, that one desperate and reckless act had led to so much destruction. Mr. Nelson was still alone in the alley. Eddie was somewhere with the Assata kids, and Bitter still didn't know how she would tell her friend that they'd left him there, with only Alex's jacket and no breath in his chest. Theron was dead, and none of them knew what that meant, if that was justice, if that would make anything better for anyone. They had all been trying to fix things in their own ways, but this? Whatever this was, wherever they had all landed, this had given them no answers, no solutions. All they had now were broken worlds and shattered stories.

Vengeance was backing away from Miss Virtue, and Bitter could see calculation simmering in its yellow eyes. Miss Virtue—the *angel* that used to be Miss Virtue—was hovering in the air, all her eyes fixed on Vengeance. It was an impossible tableau; one angel made of smoke and ash and Bitter's bloody wants, crouched low and wary with survival in its eyes, while the other angel floated like a sharp point ready to strike, many-eyed stone and still protecting the students

231

she loved. Vengeance had tried to kill Miss Virtue. Only one angel was going to leave the atrium alive, and though it was instantly clear to Bitter that the atrium and the humans inside most likely wouldn't survive the fallout, this fact seemed to have escaped Miss Virtue. Bitter was fairly certain that at this point Vengeance just didn't care.

Miss Bilphena started hustling the Assata and Eucalyptus kids back into the safety of the house, her voice low and urgent. The two angels were fixated on each other, and the air around them was beginning to sound an insistent discordant note.

"I have to stop them," Bitter said out loud, the words falling from her mouth unexpectedly.

Aloe's hand tightened around hers. "Can you?" He sounded scared, and Bitter didn't blame him. Fear was a fist around her heart, clamping it painfully.

"I have to try," she said. Blessing and Alex came up to them, and Blessing wrapped her arms around Bitter.

"We're here, babes. Idk how any of this shit works, but if you can find a way to make them stop, you gotta."

Alex nodded grimly. "The little kids are upstairs. These two could take down the whole safe house."

"Miss Virtue wouldn't," Aloe said, his voice wavering. "She loves us, even if she was lying. She wouldn't hurt us."

Bitter looked over at him. "I doh think that's Miss Virtue

anymore," she said softly, and it hurt her chest to see his face fall.

Ube rolled up to them as the last of the others filed out of the atrium. "I don't think so either," he said. Sunflower walked behind him, her face calm. Ube looked at Bitter. "Think you can get 'em to back off? We officially got too many angels in Lucille right now. They gotta get the fuck outta here."

"I don't think Vengeance will listen to me anymore," Bitter replied.

Sunflower chuckled, and the sound was out of place, disjointed. She put a hand on Bitter's shoulder, and Bitter looked up into her dark eyes. Specks of light seemed to float deep within them as Sunflower leaned down to whisper in her ear. "You can close the gate," Sunflower said, then she straightened and glanced up through the roof of the atrium. "I have to go tend to my shields." She gave Bitter an easy smile before releasing her shoulder. "Good luck, little one." As Bitter stared in confusion, Sunflower turned and left in a flurry of crisp black.

"What did she say?" Aloe asked, but Bitter didn't answer, Sunflower's words echoing in her head. What did closing the gate mean? If the angels had come in through the work, then was that how were they going to leave? Would closing the gate leave them trapped in Lucille? Or did Sunflower mean closing the gate *behind* them so they couldn't come back to this world again? A familiar spike of panic started in Bitter, but she refused to let it take root. She didn't know what she had to do, but she knew she had to do something, and she had to do it fast. The two angels were making small advances at each other, hisses and growls lacerating the air around them.

Bitter closed her eyes and stopped thinking of Vengeance as an angel. It was a painting. It was a smash of smoke trapped inside a piece of wood. It was something she had *made*, it was hers, to make alive and to make . . . unalive. It was eggshell and ash, casein and chalk, wax and blood. It had taken this form because she painted it that way, had climbed out of the panel because she *told* it to. A small suspicion began to blossom in Bitter's mind. Back in the alley, as she'd knelt weeping beside Mr. Nelson, Vengeance had been with the rest of the angels. It clearly didn't care about Mr. Nelson, but it had come when she'd called for it. That was the rule with the things Bitter made. They came when they were called. They *obeyed*.

A wild epiphany shot through Bitter. That was it; that was the key she had been missing. Her creatures obeyed her. Vengeance had come to that alley because she had told it to. She was not just a gate; *she was the gatekeeper.*

Bitter took a step forward, knowledge buzzing at the back

of her neck like effervescent lightning. Aloe tried to grab her arm, but she shook him off.

"Vengeance!" she called, her voice steadier than she'd expected. The angel snaked its long neck in her direction, seven eyes burning, and Bitter reminded herself that it was a painting, it was a thing she had made. "You eh want me to know, ent?"

Miss Virtue frowned, dust dripping off her stone brow. "Know what, child?"

Bitter didn't take her eyes off her angel. *Her* angel. The one she had made and called, the one she could command. "Yuh doh want me to know what I could do. This whole time you been here, you probably hoping I go never find out."

Vengeance slithered to her with uncanny speed, eating up the distance between them and dropping its face to hers, mouth stretching in threat. Bitter heard Aloe and Blessing gasp behind her, but she didn't turn, didn't flinch. "Careful, child," Vengeance hissed. "Your world is full of monsters."

Bitter wasn't afraid anymore. If there had been a miracle in any of this, then surely that had to be it, that she wasn't afraid anymore. All the terrors Lucille held, they were nothing compared to what she had pulled out from her heart, what she had brought to life with her monster blood, her father's stain, her mother's legacy. Vengeance was a part of her, born from her wants, just like it had said. But she wasn't trapped. There was always a choice, there was always time to realize that you had been so very wrong, and yes, there would always be costs. Next summer, there would be no Mr. Nelson handing her a carefully grown watermelon like it was a precious secret. Time was strange that way. There could be time and it could be too late, all at the same time. Bitter knew what she had to do.

"Do *not* move," she said, then she placed her hand carefully on top of the angel's scaled head. Vengeance's smoke rippled violently, but it didn't move. It narrowed all its eyes, its mouth distorted, and growled so hard that the ground of the atrium shook. Bitter didn't take her hand off its head.

"Bitter, what are you *doing*?" Aloe had both Blessing and Alex holding him back.

Bitter glanced at him and smiled, stroking her hand over the angel's scales. They had their own heat to them, something damp and thick. It was hard to believe that she'd painted them, but she remembered each small curve. "Don't worry, Aloe."

"Foolish little gate," Vengeance hissed. "We are trying to save you."

Bitter felt like she was floating. Miss Virtue had come

236

down to the ground and was watching curiously, her head tilted to one side. "I can kill it for you, child."

Bitter shook her head. "I doh need you to." She could sense tangible energy from Vengeance, dangerous tendrils that just wanted to hunt and hunt, all reaching into Lucille and connected to the other angels that were out there. "Maybe we don't need you to save us," she told it. "Maybe we can save ourselves."

Vengeance made a high-pitched clicking sound that managed to be full of derision. "Your own history proves otherwise, child."

Bitter shrugged. "Then we will make another history." She could feel the rightness of what she was doing, and it spread calm in her like a sweeping wind. Bitter closed her eyes and imagined Vengeance being sucked back into the charred wood panel it had come out of, being snapped back into whatever realm it had come out of. It was time. None of her creatures could stay here forever. "Leave our world," she commanded. "Your hunt is over."

Vengeance let out an enormous roar and lunged at her, its mouth unhinging as if to swallow Bitter alive. Aloe screamed and Miss Virtue took a rumbling step forward, but then Vengeance blew apart in a cloud of white smoke, eggshells crashing to the ground, ash layering over Bitter's clothes and eyelashes, wax melting on her sweats.

Just like that, the angel was gone.

Aloe ran up to Bitter and patted her over. "Did it hurt you?" he asked, his voice frantic. "Are you okay?"

Bitter opened her eyes and coughed, brushing ash and paint dust off her face. "I'm okay," she said. Aloe hugged her tightly, and Bitter looked over his shoulder at Miss Virtue, at the creature that used to be Miss Virtue, at the fallen angel that was maybe still Miss Virtue. "Is everything going to be okay now? Since I sent it back?"

Miss Virtue's wings rustled against each other, and her many eyes blinked. "I didn't know gates could do that."

"Sunflower told me."

Miss Virtue folded her wings in. "Sunflower and I will have a talk, then." She looked at Bitter, and Bitter felt a faint jolt of shock at the reminder that the principal had been an angel all along, masked inside a human body. How many lies was Eucalyptus built on? She was too exhausted to process it, but she could dimly recall the emotion in Miss Virtue's voice when she spoke about her students. Maybe some things were true, then. "You did well, little gate," the remaining angel said. "We shall fix the rest of it." Behind her, the mayor was still slumped on the floor, unconscious.

"Okay. Good." Bitter felt a massive wave of grayness break over her, heavy and suffocating. Vengeance was gone. Theron was dead. Lucille was still burning. Someone still had to tell Eddie about Mr. Nelson.

"Bitter?" Aloe patted her cheek. "Bitter, are you okay?"

She could feel her eyes rolling up into the back of her head, the atrium blurring around her, a soft and enveloping darkness stretching over her, and Bitter had no desire to fight it. She had already done enough. She had already done too much. With Aloe's voice fading in her ears, she let herself fall into the black.

CHAPTER 16

The first person Bitter saw when she woke up was Eddie, sitting on the edge of the bed, half her face mottled and bruised and bandaged under a curtain of braids. Bitter's head was ringing, and she felt dizzy. She tried to sit up, but Eddie shoved her back into the pillow gently. They were in the tangerine room at the safe house.

"Chill. Aloe would kill me if I let you get up. You been out all night."

Bitter sank back without a fight. She felt utterly drained, and an image of Vengeance's roaring mouth kept replaying in her head. Eddie held a glass of water up to her lips, and Bitter took a careful sip, then cleared her throat.

"So . . . yuh talking to me now?" she asked.

It was a harsh thing to start with—she hadn't even said anything to Eddie about losing her eye—but Eddie was also the last person Bitter had expected to wake up to. It felt like there was a world of hurt and guilt yawning open in her chest.

She glanced at Eddie's face and relented a little. "Shouldn't you be in bed too?"

Eddie put the glass down. "Yeah, but I wanted to see you." She sounded about as exhausted as Bitter felt.

"I real sorry," Bitter managed to say. "About . . . everything."

Eddie's voice was light. "Shit, you're not the one who shot me or Mr. Nelson."

"They told you." Bitter closed her eyes, then snapped them open again. "Wait, he was shot?"

"Yeah, they think it was a stray from the police."

"Is he still in the alley?" Bitter's chest tightened as she asked the question. She couldn't bear to think of him lying there, cold and alone for so long.

"No, no." Eddie shook her head quickly, like she could feel that abandoned horror too. "We got him out. He's home now, on the farm."

Bitter forced back the sob that threatened to accompany her words. "I'm so sorry, Eddie. I wish we could've done more for him." She didn't know if Eddie knew how she had failed at making Vengeance save Mr. Nelson, but she couldn't help feeling guilty. Eddie had taken her to this man's house and then Bitter had called an angel and now, Eddie would never smile with Mr. Nelson in his kitchen again.

Eddie shrugged, a spasm of pain crossing her face. "It's war, right? People get hurt. People die."

Bitter wanted to ask how his wife was doing, how *Eddie* was doing, but Eddie wasn't quite meeting her eyes.

"Yuh okay?" Bitter asked. Eddie nodded and twisted her hands but still didn't look at Bitter.

"You were right back then, you know," she said, changing the subject abruptly. "Not about me resenting you, but that we live in different worlds. It wouldn't have worked out."

Bitter frowned. "Why yuh bringing that up?"

"To explain," Eddie answered. "Why I don't think we can be friends, not really."

A pang of hurt shot through Bitter. She should've known. Eddie had lost too much and Bitter had made things worse and now she was losing Eddie again. "Look, I know the whole angel thing was my fault, but I was—"

"Nah, it's not even that." Eddie let her hands fall still. "You were trying to help, B. I know that." She let out a sigh and looked away. "It's because you're not Assata. I just— I need to be around people who know what it's like, especially now. It helps me feel less lonely. I didn't talk to you earlier because you wouldn't get it, how it feels to be out there, what the costs are, all that shit. And it's not your fault—you don't have to. I just . . . I just need to be around people like me."

Bitter didn't know what to say. She'd *been* out there, with

242

the angels running wild, and she'd paid costs too, but Eddie seemed to be talking about something different. The words should have hurt way more than they did, but there was so much pain inside her that this particular rejection wasn't registering the way she'd expected it to. Maybe there was only so much pain a heart could process at once, and now she was too numb to fight for her friend. Or maybe, there was nothing left to fight for, nothing she could give Eddie that would make Eddie feel safe and seen. "So yuh girlfriend, she's Assata?" All Bitter could remember was Eddie describing her as a baking and gardening type.

"Malachite? Yeah, she used to be. Like Alex. Tapped out a couple of months ago, but she knows what it's like." A semblance of light returned to Eddie's face. "We're gonna go out to this community farm she's setting up for the Elders and anyone who needs to tap out."

Bitter tried to feel something, but all she could come up with now was cold and empty space. "That sounds lovely. You should go rest out there. You deserve it." She wondered if her words sounded as manufactured as they felt, but she did care deeply about Eddie, so they were probably true. They just belonged to a Bitter she couldn't quite reach in that moment.

Someone knocked at the door, and Eddie stood up, wincing slightly. Bitter realized she was in more pain than she was showing. "I'm real sorry, B," Eddie said. "I wish shit was different."

"I real sorry, too." Bitter pulled up a smile. "Thanks for being my friend while you could."

Eddie smiled back, but it didn't reach her remaining eye. She left the room as Ube entered, wearing a light blue caftan, his hair damp as he exchanged nods with Eddie. "Good, you're awake," he said to Bitter. Eddie closed the door behind her. "How are you feeling?"

"Like I just banished an angel," Bitter replied, and Ube laughed, the sound dripping deep and sweet through the room. "What happened to the rest of them?"

"All the gates sent them back," he answered. "It was easy once they figured out you were right, the angels have to do what y'all say." Ube shook his head. "It was some spectacular shit. Between that and Miss Virtue? Whew."

Bitter wasn't sure she was ready to talk about Miss Virtue, but she had to ask. "Is she . . . okay?"

"Yeah, she's back in human form. The other form only lasted for a few hours, but it was more than enough to get shit done." He wheeled himself to the window and looked out. "A lot of shit done."

Bitter wriggled up a bit, curious. "Like what?"

Ube turned and grinned. "Like getting the mayor to appoint a new council."

"Yuh joking. Already?"

"Swear down. I ain't never seen a man that scared in my life. He pissed himself twice." Ube laughed. "But he agreed to all our terms. The city's gonna seize and redistribute Theron's assets, revamp the council to be more representative of the people, and yeah, shake things around." His grin faded. "Feels like even with everything, the work is just starting in some ways, you know. It's gonna be rough making this stick. Theron wasn't the only problem, and the other elites are gonna fight back because their shit's gonna get seized too, but I'm still counting this as a win."

"That makes sense," Bitter said, slowly processing the information, the new Lucille that was trying to form itself into existence. "It's always been bigger than one person."

"For sure. It's a whole system. We just burned it to the ground, and now we building something better back up. I think Miss Bilphena even negotiated getting some Assata Elders on the new council."

"For true?" Making Assata a part of Lucille's governance was an enormous leap, but then again, inhuman progress could be made on the backs of angels. Bitter just wasn't sure it was worth the costs, even with all the good news Ube was bringing. None of it would resurrect Mr. Nelson.

Ube scoffed. "It wasn't much of a negotiation with Miss

Virtue terrifying the crap out of him. He ain't never gonna look at her the same."

"I doh think any of us will," Bitter muttered. "How many people died?"

Ube's face sobered up even more. "It wasn't your fault, Bitter."

That didn't matter. She needed to know; it had been lying in wait in the back of her mind, the looming possibility of uncountable losses. "How many, Ube?"

He sighed. "We're not sure. The angels bust into Theron's offices to get him, and part of the building collapsed. The city's still dealing with the scene, but we lost civilians there, plus Theron's entire security detail was killed." Ube stopped and looked over at her. "This is shit that usually wouldn't leave Assata, Bitter. I need you to understand that."

Bitter nodded. "And the cops?"

A muscle jumped in his jaw. "Plainclothes shoot-out down by the north bridge. Five civilians died. We don't know that the angels were involved in that one particularly, but with those fires and shit, everything was pure fucking chaos. We don't have the body count for the cops themselves, but we know the angels took out a lot of them when they tried to interfere."

Counting Mr. Nelson, that meant at least six innocent people had died since Bitter called Vengeance into existence. She exhaled a sharp burst of air from deep in her stomach, then pushed her feelings aside. "We cyah tell other people how the angels came through, Ube. Cyah risk this happening again."

"Yeah, me and Miss Virtue talked about that. It's better if people just think the angels are Assata's angels, you know? The truth is something we have to protect right now."

"But . . . everyone saw them in the park," Bitter pointed out.

"You'd be surprised at how people can be convinced to revise their memories," Ube said, his eyes shadowing. "Miss Virtue said to leave it to her. All Assata has to do is take responsibility and the new story will stick."

Bitter stared at him. "The new story that one of you just . . . broke Theron's neck in public? Yuh okay with that?"

He nodded. "Shit, better that than what really happened, feel me?"

Bitter could feel the weight of what this decision meant at a moment like this. It would be a lie. It would be a secret they would all have to keep for the rest of their lives. Her chest felt tight and heavy. "Everyone else agreed?"

Ube gave her a look. "They're all Assata. They all know what needs to be done for Lucille to move on. As far as anyone's concerned, the angels never happened, Bitter." Even though it was a lie, a fantasy, the sound of it still sent a wave of relief through her. It must have shown in her face, because Ube took her hand and held it firmly in his. "It's over, Bitter. Try to put all this behind you, and if you're gonna remember anything, remember that at the end, you made a real difference."

Her head was still ringing. "I did?"

Ube smiled sadly. "Don't you get it? The revolution *won*. We won with blood in the streets, yeah, but still, it's everything we've been fighting for. You know how long Assata's been working for this, preparing for this? You calling Vengeance out tipped the scales."

"We could've won another way," Bitter countered. "Yuh knew from the beginning that the angels were a bad idea. People died, Ube."

He nodded slowly. "I don't like how we ended up here, Bitter. But the fact is, we're here now. All we can do is move forward."

That didn't make her feel any better. "I real hate this feeling," she said. She couldn't explain it out loud, but it was sickening, a rot in her heart, guilt in her hands, stinging tears buried in the backs of her eyes.

Ube gave her a gentle look, but it had the grit of iron behind it. "All freedoms are terrible," he said. "That's the part they never tell you."

For a moment, he sounded just like an angel.

- - - -

Aloe didn't come in until later in the afternoon. Bitter almost leaped out of bed to hug him, but he threw himself on her first, and they both laughed as they wrapped around each other, their joy edged and frayed. She rested her head on his chest, listening to his heart beat inside his ribs.

"I so glad yuh okay."

Aloe stroked her head. "Same. I wasn't sure we were going to make it out of all this." He sighed and turned to touch his forehead to hers. "I decided that I'm not going to work with Assata anymore." He said it like he'd long since decided, but had been waiting to say it out loud so it could become real.

Bitter leaned up on her elbow so she could look into his face. "Why not? Yuh love that work, and from what Ube said, they still have a lot of work to do. Don't they need you?"

Aloe was staring at the ceiling. "I need myself more, and besides, I don't have to be with Assata to heal." His voice shook a little, and Bitter could hear something tense and angry behind it.

"What's wrong?" she asked, slightly afraid of what she might find in his answer.

He shrugged. "I'm just tired. Fuck the frontline shit. You know they still don't have a count of how many people died while the angels were here?"

At least six, but definitely more, Bitter thought, with a pang of sour guilt. "Ube told me they're still figuring it out."

"You were right not to hunt with them." Aloe looked at her, and his eyes were small storms. "I'm sorry I didn't understand."

She ran her fingertips over his cheek. "Doh worry about it. It's okay now."

"Nah." He shook his head, and his eyes slid away from hers. "It's really not. I spent this morning patching up a bunch of kids who were at the park. Their parents didn't understand what the angel was about to do, and they got banged up in what was lowkey a stampede afterwards. You know how much therapy they're going to need? I can't do this anymore." Aloe paused for a moment too long. "I don't know if I'm going to stay at Eucalyptus either."

Bitter had been trying to think of how best to comfort him when she felt so bereft herself, but at that, she jerked away in surprise. "What? Why?"

"I'm thinking of transferring to a regular school. Maybe I can become, like, a nurse or a paramedic or something. Don't really wanna be a doctor, but I want to be close to the people."

Bitter was confused and starting to feel betrayed. He wasn't making sense. "How is that different from leaving

Assata if yuh just going to do the same shit? Why you need to leave Eucalyptus to do it?"

Aloe sat up, annoyed. "It's not the same shit if I'm helping civilians. They're the ones getting fucked over the most when shit like this happens."

Panic flurried up inside Bitter, ignoring her attempts to tamp it down. If he was leaving the school, what did that mean for them? Was she also part of this world he was trying to leave? She couldn't gather the courage to ask him that.

"I just need some time to think about things," Aloe was saying. "I'm going to go with Eddie to that farm her girlfriend's working on, just for a little bit."

"What? Yuh leaving?" He was leaving, not just Eucalyptus, but her. He was leaving her right when she needed him most, leaving her just like Eddie, leaving *with* Eddie, in fact.

Aloe didn't seem to notice the hurt in her voice. "It'll be a few days, max."

Bitter couldn't believe what she was hearing. "You eh even talk to me about it!"

"Bitter, you were unconscious for a whole night! And I was right here the whole time, right by your side. I just need to go take care of myself now." Aloe frowned, looking upset. "I didn't think I needed your permission for that. I thought you'd understand."

His words made sense, but Bitter couldn't stop, couldn't take them in. With all the secrets about Eucalyptus and Miss Virtue out, with Eddie walking away and Mr. Nelson dead and a rising death count all because she'd asked for Vengeance? She felt horribly unmoored, like all her anchors had dissolved into the water and now Aloe was pushing her boat out to sea.

"So yuh just going to walk away? Real supportive behavior." Her voice was so caustic, she could barely recognize it.

Aloe flinched and pulled away from her, getting up from the bed. "I've had your back this whole time, Bitter, through everything. Even after you called up an angel and didn't tell me shit. I put my feelings aside because you were going through it and you needed me." He grabbed his jacket from the bed. "Just because I take care of everyone doesn't mean I don't deserve to be taken care of too, Bitter. I'm going to let you rest."

"Aloe, wait—"

He glanced at her from the doorway, already halfway out. "I love you, but I can't do this right now. I'll see you in a few days."

The door shut with a solid click behind him, and Bitter stared at it in shock for several seconds before curling up in the unfamiliar bed and dissolving into sobs.

- - - - -

When Bitter finally returned to Eucalyptus, it was a blazing relief to her. She'd never been so eager to be back in her room. Blessing and Alex had cleaned it up before her arrival, getting rid of the charred panel Vengeance had come through, rearranging the furniture, and filling the room with fresh flowers so the space could feel like something safe when Bitter reentered it. They changed her sheets to a flowered cotton set from the linen closet and filled her pillows with lavender. Bitter hugged her friends tightly when she saw it all; then the girls waited as she took a shower for an hour, standing numbly as the hot water blasted around her. When she came out, Blessing shaved her head and patted it dry with rose water before Bitter climbed into bed. "That's enough from allyuh," she said. "I good from here."

"You sure you gonna be okay?" Blessing asked.

Bitter squeezed her hand. "Yuh done too much, even. Please go and rest." As supportive as Blessing tried to be, she couldn't hide the dark circles under her eyes and the sadness that had settled into the bones of her face. Alex looked worn out and close to fracture; all of them had paid a toll. They hugged Bitter and left, and Bitter pulled her covers over her head as soon as they were gone. She still hadn't heard from Aloe.

She stayed like that for the next few days, only leaving her bed to take perfunctory showers and eat once in a while.

Blessing kept checking on her over text, and Bitter kept lying that she was doing great, insisting that her best friend stay cocooned with Alex. It would be better for Blessing that way, to be in the arms of the person who loved her. She didn't need to be babysitting Bitter, and Bitter didn't need anyone's help. Her part in the revolution was done, bloody and complete.

Everything now was up to someone else: the restructuring of Lucille, the dismantling of the police department and prisons, the seizing and reallocation of stolen resources. Alex had been sending her updates, which Bitter read but didn't reply to because there was nothing to say, really. She had called an angel and then she'd sent it back. Theron was dead, as if by an extension of her hand. It meant that people were safer—those who had survived the angels' visit—but it also felt like her palms were stained with blood, so Bitter stayed in bed. She hid from the rest of the world, curled up against the knowledge of what she had called forth and what it had done.

On the fifth day, Miss Virtue came in and sat on the edge of Bitter's bed. Her hair was loose, reaching out into the air in tight steel curls. She smelled different, like the bottom of a river. "How are you feeling today?" she asked.

Bitter pulled her covers tighter around herself, her face

pressed close to the wall. "Fine," she lied. She couldn't bring herself to look at Miss Virtue, even though she knew the woman—the angel? the fallen angel?—was on her side. Miss Virtue's true form was seared into Bitter's brain, breathing gray stone, a resurrected sculpture with eight wings and eyes at the tip of each. How much about the principal had been a lie? Had she meant the things she'd told Bitter over the years?

"Aloe's here," Miss Virtue said.

Bitter sat up so fast that it made her head spin, all concerns about Miss Virtue shoved to the side. "What? When did he come back?"

Miss Virtue hid a smile and smoothed her hands over her suit. Her nails were blood red against the dark mossy green. "Last night. He's out in the hall, but he's not sure if you want to see him."

Bitter tried to ignore how ferociously her heart was pounding in her chest and the way her whole being tugged toward the door now that she knew Aloe was on the other side of it. "He thinks ah vex with him?"

Miss Virtue raised an eyebrow. "Well, from what he told me, it sounds like you *were* a bit vexed that he left."

Bitter hung her head. "I was being petty. He deserved to take some time for himself. I just—I eh wanna lose him how I lose Eddie."

"Sometimes we have to trust that the ones we love will find their way back to us," Miss Virtue replied.

Bitter glanced over at her. The air between them had changed ever since Miss Virtue split into stone. "What happens now?" Bitter asked in a low voice. "With the school?" She'd been wondering this for days, ever since she learned the truth about Eucalyptus, but she'd been too scared to go looking for the answer. She and the others had fulfilled their function by closing the gates—did that mean the school would shut down?

Miss Virtue smiled. "Eucalyptus will be here as long as there are students who need it," she answered. "Until the humans have made Lucille into a place where a school like this isn't needed anymore."

Bitter scoffed. "How long that go take?"

"As long as it takes, little gate." Miss Virtue touched Bitter's chin affectionately, and to Bitter's surprise, the contact didn't make her flinch. "You made a good call, you and Ube, about keeping what really happened under wraps. The world is never ready for the real angels. And now your children will grow up in a Lucille you won't even recognize."

Bitter searched the principal's eyes, not sure what she was looking for. "It won't be the same here," she said. "At the school. Even if you try not to change it."

Miss Virtue tilted her head. "It *shouldn't* be the same. I made the choices I made to keep you in the dark, but we can all make different choices." She gave another smile, this one tinged with sadness. "I broke your trust, Bitter. And the trust of the other students. I will spend as long as it takes to rebuild it."

Bitter nodded, a knot in her chest loosening up a bit. She knew what it was like to keep a secret that was so big, no one would have believed it without seeing it themselves. She could understand why the principal had hidden her wings and stone from them, but everything was still raw and scary and starting over.

"I just want to be safe." She tried to stop her fear from leaking into her voice, but it made it through anyway, lacing her words with the shadow of a tremble.

"Oh, Bitter. You are always safe here." Miss Virtue held out her arms, and Bitter fought back tears as she hugged the fallen angel for the first time. Miss Virtue felt solid, almost unnaturally so, like the stone of her being was translating into the flesh, but her embrace was warm and sure. "I will stay with Eucalyptus," she said, her voice washing like an ocean of promise into Bitter's ear. "I have always known that you kids were worth a forever, but now it's time for me to prove that I can be a forever for you."

Bitter's voice was muffled. "Wait, yuh immortal?"

Miss Virtue laughed. "Human forevers are shorter, Bitter. There will come a time when you won't need me anymore."

Bitter took a deep breath, her face pressed against the shoulder of Miss Virtue's moss suit. "And then you'll leave?"

"And then I will leave, little gate, like everyone else must. But that is many, many years from now." Miss Virtue pulled away and wiped the tears off Bitter's face. "You were very brave to send Vengeance back. I am so proud of you. Just . . . no more blood, okay?"

Bitter laughed through a sniffle. "No more secrets, then."

"Deal." Miss Virtue stood up, her suit still somehow uncreased and immaculate. "Make sure you go down for dinner tonight. The chef refuses to continue your room delivery. He says he misses your face."

Bitter nodded and watched as the principal left, then stared at the doorway with an unsteady chest until Aloe's frame filled the blank space. His eyes crinkled when he saw her, love and relief glowing like everlasting embers in his face. "Hey, Bitter," he said.

She teared up at the sound of his voice. "Hey," she said back, her voice unsteady.

Aloe was a shade darker than when he'd left, his skin smoothed out by the sun. "Can I come cuddle with you?"

Bitter nodded, words too thick for her tongue. Aloe

nudged off his shoes, then took off his jacket and climbed into the bed with her. She let out a deep breath as he wrapped his arms around her and pulled her close. He smelled like lemons and outside. "I'm sorry I had to leave," he whispered. "I wasn't abandoning you."

"I know. Sorry I gave you a hard time. I was scared you wouldn't come back."

Aloe kissed the top of her head. "I'll always come back for you, Bitter. We in this together."

For a moment, she thought about the things he'd said at the safe house, about leaving Eucalyptus and doing something else. But just as quickly, Bitter decided it didn't matter where he went. She could feel her love for him as clearly as if it was setting her heart on fire. If he wanted to change schools, then fine. There was a world outside Eucalyptus's walls, and she had already survived the worst of it. All Bitter wanted was the exact same thing she had wanted before— peace and quiet. Her friends around her. Aloe's smile in her mornings. The only difference was that she now knew precisely how high the price of that was, how the costs could be bled out of you.

"You doh have to stay at Eucalyptus for me," she told him. "I want you to do what makes you happy, even if that means going somewhere else." Bitter looked down at his face, his patient and gentle eyes, his gorgeous mouth. "I want to take care of you, Aloe. I want to give you somewhere safe and soft to rest, just like you does do for me."

Aloe leaned over and kissed the tip of her nose. "I'm not going anywhere. I decided to stay."

Bitter blinked in confusion and frowned, hesitant to believe what he was saying. "Yuh sure? Yuh not just saying that for me?"

Aloe rolled his eyes. "Babe, I'm sure."

Joy spilled in Bitter's chest like paint, seeping into all the crevices and leaking out of her smile. "How come?" she asked, because she had to be certain.

Aloe shrugged. "I definitely needed to get away to the farm, and it helped me see that we have *time* now, you know? Like, I think I know how I want to help people, but I have time to figure it out. We have time to imagine whatever we want and make it real. That's the Lucille we live in, that's what we can give to ourselves and each other."

Bitter gazed into his face. He was so wholesome, so eager to give back to the people he cared about and even those he didn't know. "Yuh real important to me, you know?"

Aloe laughed, the sound bubbling up through his teeth. "Bitter, you are my whole heart. I wish I could tell our kids everything about you one day."

She poked his ribs, even as her heart soared at how easily

he made it sound like they would have decades together. "Doh you dare. We all agreed: none of this happened."

"Yeah, yeah. A new world, a clean start." He tangled his fingers up with hers.

Bitter had never been the one who said the romantic things in their relationship. That was always Aloe, the dreamer, the soft and hopeful one. But in these days, her feelings were clear and precise, and she was no longer afraid. "I'll love you in any world," she whispered. "I promise."

Aloe stroked her cheek and leaned in to kiss her. "I'm going to hold you to that," he whispered back, his words brushing against her breath.

Bitter closed her eyes and chose to dream with him. Lucille was gone, Lucille was being born, made anew in the hands of the people. Outside the window, faint thrills of ash floated through the air.

ACKNOWLEDGMENTS

Writing this book was one of the hardest things I've ever had to do, what with the pandemic, escalating civil unrest, and a body that has become progressively more disabled over the past few years. I am endlessly grateful to every single person who fed my discipline throughout the years, because that rigor is what got me through. As always, I could not make this work without the community that holds me up.

To Katherine Agyemaa Agard, for literally typing for me, week after week, over Zoom sessions, when I lost the ability to write or use a keyboard. I can never tell you how much it meant. Thank you so much.

To Ann Daramola, for loving this book, asking the best questions, and reminding me to send them back for Mr. Nelson. Thinking through books with you is a genuine honor and a gift.

To Yagazie Emezi, who has built worlds with me all my

life, for helping me make angels real, forming Vengeance with me, and choosing its voice.

To Bilphena Yahwon and Nnennaya Amuchie, for teaching me about better worlds from the work I witness you doing in this one.

To Gwendolyn Brooks, Assata Shakur, and Mariame Kaba, for your work and your words.

To the Black radical communities committed to our liberation, thank you, thank you, thank you. I hope these stories help.